MURDER AT KENSINGTON GARDENS

A COZY HISTORICAL MYSTERY

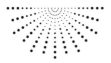

LEE STRAUSS

BROWN BOOKS
PUBLISHING GROUP

GINGER GOLD MYSTERIES

(IN ORDER)

MURDER AT KENSINGTON GARDENS

A Ginger Gold Mystery

Book 6

By Lee Strauss

Murder at Kensington Gardens

Brown Books Publishing Group

16250 Knoll Trail Drive, Suite 205

Dallas, Texas 75248

www.BrownBooks.com

(972) 381-0009

A New Era in Publishing®

ISBN 978-1-61254-999-6

LCCN 2017964727

Printed in the United States

10 9 8 7 6 5 4 3 2 1

For more information or to contact the author, please go to

www.leestraussbooks.com

CHAPTER ONE

"*Y*our wife isn't being unfaithful, Mr. Pattison." Mrs. Ginger Gold, also known as Lady Gold, produced photographs taken with her new camera. "She's been visiting her grandmother at St. Olave's Hospital."

"Well, ain't that a kettle of fish." Mr. Pattison, a slender middle-aged man with a soft belly and thinning hair, clearly was insecure with his younger wife. "The old bat never approved of our marriage. It was a nasty affair with harsh words spoken between us. She vowed never to speak to Mrs. Pattison again, and I'd forbidden the wife from further communication."

"It seems Mrs. Pattison wanted to set things right between them before her grandmother passes away. I hope you will go easy on her, Mr. Pattison. In my opinion, it shows a quality of character."

Mr. Pattison sighed. "I suppose you're right. It's

certainly preferable to the alternative. Thank you for your exemplary service, Lady Gold."

Ginger accepted her payment and wished Mr. Pattison a good day. The spring weather—typically dreary and damp— offered a rare showing of the sun. Ginger enjoyed a drive through the streets of London in her new ivory Crossley motorcar. Her black and white Boston terrier slept on the soft red leather of the passenger seat, his ears pointing to the roof when Ginger opened the door.

"Another case solved, Bossy," she said as she slid in. "This private investigative work is going swimmingly."

Ginger had officially taken on the role of private investigator two months previously. Her first case had been a murder, and she was glad the ones that had kept her busy these last few weeks were far less serious. Domestic issues, lost items, missing persons. So far she had solved every one and in good time. Ginger acknowledged that working for the British secret service during the Great War had trained her well for such tasks.

Ginger arrived at St. George's Church just as her good friend, Reverend Oliver Hill, returned from a stroll through the parish gardens. The young vicar, a tall, lanky fellow with a ready smile, was only thirty-three. He jogged to the Crossley in order to open Ginger's door. His blue-green eyes sparkled as he greeted her. "Ginger, hello!"

Ginger placed her gloved hand in his and allowed

him to assist her out of the motorcar. "Good afternoon, Oliver."

"So nice to see you," Oliver said with obvious joy. In the sun, his red hair rivaled Ginger's. "What brings you to St. George's?"

"I'm hoping you can give me a bit of advice."

"I'd be delighted to try. Would you like to come in for tea? I believe Mrs. Davies has a pot ready."

"That would be splendid." Ginger called for her little dog. "You don't mind if Boss joins us?"

"Of course not. Boss is always welcome here."

St. George's Church, City of London, was an eighteenth-century structure built of limestone. It had a medium-sized chapel with a square tower instead of a steeple, an attached hall with a kitchen and other small rooms used for various purposes. Oliver, a bachelor, lived in the vicarage next door to the church. Ginger hadn't been inside Oliver's private quarters, but she expected they would be sparsely decorated and tidy, if she could go by Oliver's manners.

They walked along a stone path toward a side entrance through a small garden of cornflowers, yellow roses and red gerbera daisies.

"I dare say," Oliver said, looking skywards, "it's nice enough to have tea outdoors. At least until those clouds roll in."

"I know Boss is happy about the arrangement."

Oliver gave Mrs. Davies, the church's robust secretary and general manager, instructions and helped her to prepare a table outside. Oliver covered it with a white embroidered cloth and the church secretary added a vase of colorful tulips.

"They're lovely," Ginger said as she claimed a chair. Boss scampered blissfully across the garden and back, stopping to spin in a couple of circles, before tiring out and reclining at Ginger's feet.

Oliver laughed at the pup. "Poor thing doesn't have a tail to chase."

Mrs. Davies returned with a hot pot of tea accompanied by fresh crumpets.

"Those smell wonderful!" Ginger said.

"I baked them just this morning, madam."

"I can pour, Mrs. Davies," Oliver said kindly. Mrs. Davies nodded and returned to the kitchen.

Ginger sipped her tea, then said, "Any progress on your *assignment?*" Ginger's brow jumped as her lips tugged into a smile. Oliver's single status, while normally not an issue for most priests, had become a point of concern for the diocese as it had come to their attention that the single women in the parish were quite distracted. The recommendation, therefore, was for Oliver to find a wife and to do it soon.

Oliver smirked as he set his teacup down. "Well, there is a girl I'm fond of."

"Oh?" Ginger didn't want to pry, but was indeed curious. She hoped Oliver would confide in her. Waiting a moment, she let the silence between them prompt him. To her delight, he made her a confidante.

"Her name's Mary Blythe. She works as a receptionist for a dentist. She's nice."

"Just *nice*?"

"Of course, she's more than nice. She's kind, good with children, and a good cook."

Ginger lowered her chin and stared at her friend. "I'm not sensing a certain *jeune amour*. Are you sure she's the one?"

"I think so. I like her."

"But are you in love with her?"

"I'm sure that will grow with time. She'd be a suitable vicar's wife."

Ginger held in the raspberry that formed at her lips.

"I'm not about to confirm anything yet," Oliver continued. "We're hardly courting."

"My advice is not to rush your decision," Ginger said gravely. "As you know, the sacrament of marriage isn't something to be taken lightly. The rest of your life could be a really long time."

"Yes, you are correct. I just wish the diocese would put their noses somewhere else. Maybe there is another lady I've yet to notice. Pray for me, Ginger, if you think of it. The whole matter is quite distressing if one dwells on it too much."

"Of course." Ginger slathered butter onto a crumpet and took a bite. "Delicious. Mrs. Davies is a master."

"I agree most heartily," Oliver said, wiping crumbs off his chin. "I'm blessed to have her at St. George's. Anyway, enough about me. You said you'd like advice about something. How can I help?"

"Marvin Elliot will be in prison for a long time, and I'm not entirely sure how to help young Scout."

Ginger had met the orphan cousins Marvin and Scout Elliot on the SS *Rosa* when she crossed from Boston to England the previous summer. They both worked in steerage, and Scout had taken care of Boss in the kennel. Ginger had taken a shine to the cousins and once in England, often gave them small jobs to help them out financially— after all, they were too proud to accept charity. Unfortunately, Marvin had got involved with the wrong people, and Ginger had stepped in as Scout's guardian.

"I meant to ask about how the lad is faring in your care." Oliver's expression grew serious. "Forgive me."

Ginger waved the apology off. "He's doing well for the most part. Does his chores with fervor, loves Boss and my new gelding, Goldmine. The tutor says he's doing well with his studies. He's very keen on doing his very best and to please everyone."

"I'm not seeing the problem."

"That *is* the problem. He's only eleven yet sometimes he walks around like he's an old man with slumped shoulders and watery eyes. Marvin's criminal activities and incarceration weigh heavily on him."

"I see," Oliver said. "Perhaps he needs someone to talk to."

Ginger agreed. "I tell him all the time he can speak to me about Marvin, but he always shakes his head."

"He might need a man to bring it out of him. After all, he's lost the one man left in his life."

Ginger sipped her tea and considered Oliver's point. "You might be right. You don't mind seeing him?"

"Of course not! I miss the young lad. Under your tutelage, I believe he's going to grow into a fine and upright man."

Ginger smiled at this. "I hope so."

Ginger and Oliver arranged a time suitable to them both, and Ginger promised to get Clement to bring Scout over.

"Before I forget," Oliver said, "our choir is in need of new members." He grinned, "Preferably ones who can carry a tune. You have a lovely voice, Ginger. Would you consider joining?"

Ginger actually lived in the parish of Kensington, but she'd been making the journey to St. George's on Sunday mornings ever since she and the vicar had struck up a friendship over the charity they'd started together. The Child Wellness Project had been set up to help children like Scout by providing meals and clothing and general aid.

"I do miss singing in a church choir," Ginger said. "It's been years. So, yes. I'd love to join."

Oliver slapped his thighs. "Splendid!"

A telephone call came in for Oliver, so Ginger said her goodbyes and called for Boss to follow her to the Crossley.

Before starting the engine, Ginger checked her image in the rearview mirror. She smoothed out her red bob, re-enforcing the curls that looped under her high cheekbones, and straightened her mint-green turban hat. She fished through her handbag, retrieving her tangerine-blossom lipstick, applied the colour and smacked her lips together. Satisfied, she adjusted the mirror to its proper position.

If Ginger were simply returning home to Hartigan House, she wouldn't have bothered, but she was heading to Mayfair to see Basil Reed.

Her heart fluttered.

CHAPTER TWO

*A*fter almost losing Basil to a gunshot wound, Ginger's desire and affection for the chief inspector had grown deeply. Not since her love affair with her late husband, Daniel, had she felt feelings anywhere close to what she felt now.

Their last obstacle in their relationship was Basil's estranged wife, Emelia. Basil, now having sufficient proof of her adultery, was finally divorcing her.

Ginger parked in front of Basil's townhouse with anticipation. She glanced at the backseat. Lying there was a large item, square and about two inches deep, wrapped in brown paper and pink ribbon. A present for Basil.

"Come on, Bossy," Ginger said. Despite Basil's dislike of dogs—a fear originated by a biting incident when Basil was a child—Basil had warmed to Boss. Ginger had been convinced a friendship between Basil and Boss was inevitable, and she was right. She retrieved the present from the back seat and headed to the front door.

Basil opened the glossy wooden door before Ginger had a chance to knock.

Dressed in a fine, pin-striped suit, his hair—brown and sprinkled with grey at the temples, was parted sharply at the side and oiled back. He grinned at her with delight. "I saw the Crossley through the window." Then he pulled her inside and closed the door with his foot.

Boss scampered in just in time, sat next to the gift Ginger let rest against the wall, and watched with round brown eyes as his mistress wrapped her arms around Basil's neck.

Ginger loved Basil's choice in aftershave, a woodsy clean scent, and how the lines around his hazel eyes deepened as he gazed at her.

"Hello," he said before kissing her.

"Hello," she said as she kissed him back.

Boss barked and nosed Ginger's legs against the hem of her ivory net and lace dress. It was the latest in the spring fashion line with lace capped sleeves, a dropped waist with a pink silk crepe slip underneath, and a matching lace rose at one hip. She swooped down to pick the dog up. "He gets jealous," she said with laughter in her voice. "He doesn't like to be left out."

Basil grimaced. "And just when I was starting to tolerate the creature."

"He loves you, Basil. You must at least like him."

"If you insist." Basil's gaze landed on the parcel against the wall. "What's this?"

"It's a present."

Basil narrowed his gaze on Ginger. "What's the occasion? I haven't missed something, have I?"

"No, silly. It's just something I thought you might like."

They walked into the sitting room, and Ginger was suddenly nervous. Maybe this hadn't been a good idea. It was too late to back out now. She couldn't very well take the gift back. She sat on a leather-backed chair as Basil worked the wrapping paper off.

He gripped the framed painting with both hands and stared hard at the image. His eyebrows bounced up in question.

"You're giving me *The Mermaid*?"

The marbles that had formed in Ginger's stomach clinked. "Don't you like it?"

"Of course, I like it. You know I'm a fan of Waterhouse."

Ginger couldn't stop herself from glancing at another Waterhouse painting hanging on the wall.

"Only," Basil said gently, "doesn't this have sentimental value to you? You'd said it was a gift from your father to your mother."

"It was," Ginger admitted. The shimmering blue tail of the mythical mermaid curled around her creamy white torso as she sat on a rocky shore. The calm waters pooled behind her in an enclave. She brushed out long red hair whilst her emerald-eyed gaze rested on something mysterious in the distance. The painting reminded Ginger of her mother, and "by extension" of Ginger herself. When it came to Ginger's physical appearance, she had taken after her mother.

Basil's gaze scanned the room. "Now, where shall I hang it?"

Every wall of the sitting room was filled with some painting, photograph, or collectible item. Ginger strolled to the other Waterhouse called *Destiny*. The main focus was a woman who reminded Ginger of Emelia Reed, and the painting's presence made Ginger feel as if she and Basil were never alone. "I think it should go here," she said boldly.

Basil's chin notched up, but he remained silent. A knowing look registered in his eyes and Ginger was sure that he understood her real reasoning. She glanced away, feeling somewhat sheepish. *Had she gone too far?*

But then Basil spoke. "Righto." He immediately took down the *Destiny* painting and replaced it with *The Mermaid*. He made a show of taking in the new look of his wall, crossing one arm over his chest with the other hand propped under his chin. "You're right. This one is much better."

Ginger punched him lightly on the shoulder. "You're mocking me!"

Basil gathered her in his arms, and kissed her while saying, "Never."

Over the last few weeks, Ginger had grown

comfortable with Basil's embrace. At first, she couldn't help but compare him to her late husband, Daniel: the breadth of his chest, the scent of his skin, the feel of his lips. At least the sense of disloyalty she'd initially experienced was dissipating with each day.

Ginger pulled away gently and without looking into Basil's eyes said, "If you want, I can store the *Destiny* for you." She didn't want the image of Emelia to find its way to another wall in Basil's house.

"If you like," Basil said, leaning down for another kiss. Then taking her hand, he pulled her toward the gramophone. "Isham Jones?"

Ginger nodded. "Swinging Down the Lane" began to play, and Basil pulled Ginger in close, one hand in his the other on her waist, and led her around the room.

The song took her back to the cocktail lounge of the SS *Rosa*, where they'd first met. Ginger had travelled with her American companion and close friend Haley Higgins on the route from Boston to Liverpool. Basil had also been a passenger.

She hadn't yet known his name, but she'd watched him, a dapper gentleman, from across the room and wondered if he would ask her to dance. When he did, it was like they'd been dance partners all their lives. Rhythm, which came naturally to Basil, had been a struggle for her late husband, Daniel. When dancing with Basil, whether the waltz like they were doing now or the upbeat jazz-craze dance of the Charleston, it was like they were one person. Bodies and minds in harmony with each other, knowing instinctively how to move together; it was spiritual and intimate.

She felt Basil's breath near her ear. He whispered, "I love you, Ginger Gold."

Ginger's heart seemed to stop. For the first time since she'd met and danced with Basil, she lost a beat. All at once, she was both ecstatic and terrified. She knew she had to let go of Daniel. *I'll never stop loving him*, Ginger thought. But it had been six years since he died, and it was time for her to move on. Daniel would want her to. Her feelings for Basil were different, but they were true.

"I love you too, Basil Reed."

Suddenly the music faded away, and she knew of nothing more than Basil's lips and embrace. She was ready for a lifetime of this.

The telephone interrupted them, and Basil groaned.

"I have to get this," he said ruefully. Pulling out of their embrace, he went to the occasional table where a candlestick phone continued to shrill. Basil picked it up by the neck and placed the cone-shaped receiver to his ear.

"Reed, here."

After listening for a few moments, he said, "Yes, Superintendent Morris. I'll be right there."

He sighed as he returned to Ginger's side. "I'm sorry, but I'm afraid duty calls."

"A murder?"

Basil grinned. He knew that Ginger wasn't known

to stand on the sidelines of a good murder mystery. "Not so exciting as that, dear girl."

"Very well." Ginger gathered the *Destiny* under one arm and Boss under the other.

"Let me help you with that," Basil said, taking the painting. He walked Ginger to the Crossley and assisted her as she slid in. "Dinner tomorrow night?"

Ginger smiled brightly. "Absolutely!"

CHAPTER THREE

*G*inger called in at her Regent Street dress shop, Feathers & Flair. She'd leased the two-story limestone building in the autumn of the previous year. Business in the first quarter of 1924 had proven to be steady, in part because Ginger had had the foresight to stock factory-made frocks as well as the usual imports from well-known fashion houses. Ladies from the upper classes had caught on to the convenience. There were the lower prices. Plus, the luxury of shopping for a dress that fitted and returning home with it that very day was quite compelling.

Thankfully, Ginger had employees she could count on since she'd lately been spending fewer hours at the shop, now, occupied as she was, with her private detective side job, her ward, Scout Elliot, the houseful of staff and the women in her care. And then there was Boss and her newly acquired, exquisite gelding. And

16

she couldn't forget her burgeoning friendship with Basil Reed! He needed her time as well. Ginger sighed contentedly. Her life was good.

Madame Roux, Ginger's competent shop manager, was busy with a customer, smoothly answering her questions and giving reassurances as to the quality and originality of the gown of interest. Within minutes, Madame Roux had a sale. When the patron had her back turned, Ginger winked at her manager who nodded subtly with a slight twitch of the lips.

Tastefully decorated, the shop had shiny marble-tiled floors, tall white walls trimmed in gold, and electric chandeliers. Not overly stocked, there were just a few mannequins on display, a rack of scarves and accessories, and a wall dominated by hats.

"You will be the queen of the ball, Mrs. Sutton." Madame Roux's accent with the way she presented herself, neck long and shoulders back, confirmed that she was distinctly French.

Ginger carried Boss to the back room, concealing him as much as she could under one arm. She slipped through the velvet curtain that separated the back area from the front. Some customers objected to a canine presence in the shop, so Ginger tried to be as subtle as possible.

Emma was bending over a new Singer sewing machine, hands pushing fabric under the needle as her foot worked the large iron pedal underneath the wooden dock, back and forth, to keep the needle going. She was so engrossed in her creation she barely acknowledged Ginger's arrival. Boss went directly to his bed, which was kept in the back room for his occasional visits. Curling up, Boss promptly closed his eyes.

Leaving Emma to her masterpiece, Ginger returned to the front and went upstairs to the second floor. As expected, she found her employee Dorothy West, a pleasant if not emotional girl who came from a middle-class family. Her simple style suited the clientele who frequented the upper level of Feathers & Flair, since the elite generally didn't like to be shown up by a shop assistant. Dorothy was engaged with a customer. What Ginger hadn't expected, however, was that the customer would be none other than Basil's estranged wife, Emelia Reed.

Ginger's entrance caught her nemesis' attention. Emelia glanced at Ginger with contempt. "Lady Gold."

"Mrs. Reed. This is a surprise."

"Why is that? I'm in the market for a good frock as much as the next woman."

Ginger eyed her with suspicion. It wasn't like Feathers & Flair was the only upper-end dress shop. "I hope you are finding what you're looking for."

"Miss West is filling me in on the trend of factory frocks. Quite enlightening."

Dorothy blushed and pushed her shingled brown hair behind her ear. The effort accidentally knocked a hairpin onto the floor. She swooped to pick it up.

"Excuse me," she said.

"That's a beautiful pin," Emelia said with interest.

"It's a story button pin," Dorothy said. "My grand-mother's."

"What's the story?" Ginger asked, taking a glimpse at the tiny relief sculpture surrounded by a circular silver frame.

"It's Lucy and Edgardo, tragic lovers from an Italian opera."

"How intriguing!" Emelia examined it before handing it back, and Dorothy slipped it into the pocket of her fine-knit sweater.

Ginger headed back downstairs feeling unnerved by Emelia Reed's presence in her shop. She wondered if Emelia intended to ask Dorothy about Ginger's relationship with Basil. If so, Mrs. Reed would be disappointed. Ginger had never mentioned Basil to her staff as she and Basil had agreed to keep their relationship quiet until his divorce was finalized.

CHAPTER FOUR

*H*artigan House was a large house in the prosperous district of South Kensington. When George Hartigan passed away, Ginger had inherited it along with a sizable sum of money and a percentage of her father's American manufacturing business. At first, it had been only herself and her American friend Haley living in the large house, along with a small staff of three. Now it was home to not only Ginger and Haley but Ginger's grandmother-in-law, Ambrosia; her sister-in-law, Felicia; a long-term guest, Miss Matilda Hanson; and Ginger's ward, Scout Elliot.

Ginger parked the motorcar in the garage and, with Boss at her heels, strolled through the back garden to the door leading to the morning room. She found Ambrosia engrossed in the April edition of *Vogue* magazine, the cover sketch aptly portraying a sea of colorful umbrellas at the feet of two fashion-conscious women, one opening a green umbrella and the other a red, under heavy rain.

The Dowager Lady Gold's round eyes squinted in concentration, and she nearly jumped out of her skin when Ginger made her presence known.

Ambrosia snapped the magazine closed and threw it on the chair beside her. "Ginger! You startled me!"

"So sorry, Grandmother. I thought you heard me come in."

Felicia's cheerful voice trickled into the room before she entered with an enraptured Matilda Hanson at her side. Miss Hanson, a bright medical student, had the misfortune of having found herself unwed and with child, a situation sure to damn a woman to shame and poverty, even in these modern times. Ginger had offered to shelter Miss Hanson until the child came and could be adopted, much to Ambrosia's dismay. "There are homes for ruined women, you know."

"I'm looking for my magazine," Felicia said. "There's something darling inside that I just have to show Matilda."

Matilda.

Ginger was pleased that Felicia and Miss Hanson had become friendly enough to move to first names. It hadn't been so long ago that Felicia had expressed her disapproval over Miss Hanson moving in with her "tarnished reputation."

Ginger glanced at Ambrosia who shrugged a soft

shoulder. "I haven't seen it. Waste of good paper if you ask me."

Ginger chuckled. "I think I spotted it on one of the chairs."

Felicia circled the table until her gaze landed on the magazine. "Here it is." She took a chair and patted the one beside her for Matilda.

"The weather's rather tolerable," Ginger said. "I just had a pleasant tea in the gardens of St. George's Church with Reverend Hill. We could move to the veranda."

"I would but . . ." Miss Hanson's hand moved over her protruding stomach. "I'm afraid Mrs. Schofield might catch a glimpse."

Ginger had sworn the household to secrecy but could do nothing about the neighbors if they caught sight of the unmarried mother. The notoriously nosey Mrs. Schofield was not above inviting herself over to visit Ambrosia—another thing her grandmother objected to, but in this case, propriety prevented her a way out.

"Quite right. Well, you get a nice breeze in through the windows, and if you shift over slightly, you can sit in the sun's rays."

"Yes, you're right, Lady Gold. Good idea."

Ambrosia grunted as she leaned on her walking stick to stand. "I'll see myself to the drawing room." The elder Lady Gold had taken to escaping to the grand, but underused, room when Miss Hanson had moved in, "turning Hartigan House into a hostel!"

"Have you seen Haley about?" Ginger asked.

Felicia drew her attention from the magazine article. "I believe she's reading in the sitting room."

Before making her way to the sitting room, Ginger took a peek into the kitchen, hoping to find Scout there. Mrs. Beasley, Ginger's stout, no-nonsense cook, had him sweeping the floor. Even though the lad was Ginger's ward, he'd been a street urchin, and therefore of low social standing. This required Ginger bringing him in as a hired hand and the boy sleeping in the attic with the rest of the staff. She was grateful to get Scout off the streets, no matter the route it had to take.

She left him undisturbed and found Haley in the sitting room. She and Haley often shared an evening sherry or brandy together (phoo to those who said brandy was a man's drink—she'd drink it if she wanted to!), and Ginger was pleased to see that Haley had poured one for her. The cut-crystal tumbler sat a quarter full on the table beside her favorite chair.

"You're a brick, Haley," Ginger said as she eased into her chair. She removed her beaded Paul Poiret pumps —tiny colorful beads created a mini tapestry of a French village—and put her silk-stockinged feet up on the ottoman. She sipped her brandy and let out a sigh.

Haley lounged on the settee with long legs crossed at the ankles. She straightened her tweed skirt and pushed wayward dark curls back into her faux bob. "Hard day?" she asked.

"No, not really. Just busy."

"Me, too," Haley said. "Another bridge jumper."

"Oh, no."

"And a motorcar crash two deceased."

Haley had just finished her third year at London's medical school for women and had been offered an internship over the summer at University College Hospital, London's premier teaching college. Ginger had always known her friend was highly intelligent and had rejoiced when the administration chose Haley for a position that normally went to a fourth-year student and, usually, a man.

"How awful," Ginger said sincerely. She knew what it was like to lose people you loved.

The stone house could hold a chill. Thankful that someone had started a fire in the hearth, Ginger gazed at the snapping flames before shifting her focus to the empty space above the mantel.

"I'm assuming you've noticed *The Mermaid* is missing," Haley said. "I hope we haven't had a robbery."

"I removed it," Ginger admitted.

"Whatever for? I thought you loved that painting."

"Basil admired it too. I gave it to him as a gift."

Haley studied Ginger with a look of amusement. "As a reminder of you and your red hair?"

Ginger narrowed her green eyes indignantly. "You think you're so clever, Haley Higgins!"

Haley laughed. "I'm right!" She looked at the painting of the brunette in a red dress Ginger had rested against the wall. "And that's the one it replaced?"

"Yes. The figure reminds me of Emelia. I felt like she

was watching me every time I went over to Basil's house."

Haley chuckled again. "What are you going to do with the brunette now?"

"The attic. Deep in the attic." Ginger took a long sip of her brandy. "She came into the shop today. I think she means to spy on me."

"Really?" Haley said. "That's brazen."

"I thought so too. She flouted herself like she had every right and reason in the world to be there."

"Did you ask if she's signed the divorce papers?"

"If only I could be so audacious," Ginger said with a huff. "I'm too well bred, I'm afraid. I'm certain, unfortunately, that it shan't be the last I'll see of Mrs. Reed."

THE DOORBELL RANG just as Ginger left Haley in the sitting room, but Pippins was already there, answering the door. "It's the books you ordered, madam, for the library."

With all that had happened in the day, Ginger had forgotten the order from Hatchards was to arrive. She meant to restore the small library on the second floor. Grace and Lizzie had given it a good dust over, and Felicia had taken charge of the décor with new carpets, curtains, and wallpaper. The books currently shelved were mostly those that had interested her father, business and philosophy, but there were a good number of classics, and art books. Painting had been a pastime her father had dabbled in. These new books would add more recently published volumes to the collection.

Boss ran down the stairs to investigate the commotion, and Ginger whisked him up under her arm to keep him from racing outside the open door. Felicia and Miss Hanson also materialized at the top of the stairwell to quench their curiosity.

"The books are here?" Felicia asked.

Miss Hanson remained on the landing while Felicia skipped excitedly down the stairs. Ginger was grateful that Felicia had eagerly taken on the library project—a much better pastime than the questionable haunts she'd been frequenting and equally questionable characters she'd been spending time with.

"Ginger!" Felicia said with obvious glee. She'd ripped open the first box and lifted out a book. "It's Bram Stoker's *Dracula*. First edition!

Ginger frowned. "I don't remember ordering that."

"That's because I ordered it," Felicia said as she examined the book.

Ginger raised a brow. "I can hear your grandmother now. 'Not suitable reading for the young elite of the female persuasion.'"

Felicia scoffed. "What Grandmama doesn't know won't hurt her. Vampires are all the rage in London. People dress up at night and wander through Kensington Gardens to scare clandestine lovers!"

Oh, mercy.

"In fact, doesn't Kensington Palace look like a place vampires would dwell? Especially in the fog of twilight?" Felicia carried the copy upstairs to where Miss Hanson was waiting. "Have a look, Matilda."

Ambrosia's grey mop-bun head poked out from behind the drawing room doors. "What's all this noise about?" she demanded.

"Just books for the library," Felicia called down cheerfully from the top of the stairs.

Ambrosia's gaze narrowed as they reached the unwed mother who looked over the entrance hall from the landing. The elder Lady Gold hadn't made the same social evolution as her granddaughter. Despite being 'ruined,' Matilda Hanson was also a commoner. Ambrosia disappeared back into the drawing room in a huff.

CHAPTER FIVE

*T*he next morning, with the light of dawn, Ginger was roused mid-dream. She and Daniel were at a baseball game in Boston. Fenway Park had just opened, and they were cheering on their team, eating hotdogs and laughing. Ginger was in love.

Boss, awakened to movement in the bed, trotted to her side and licked her cheek.

"Good morning, boy," she said, eyes still closed. Her fingers stretched over to the bedside table in search of her wedding ring. Her eyes snapped opened, and her hand went limp. She'd put her ring away long ago. Daniel was gone. She was with Basil now.

Ginger's chest tightened, washed anew with melancholy and that dratted, lingering sense of disloyalty. *I'm not being unfaithful to Daniel. He is dead. I am legally and morally free to be with another.*

Her mind latched onto Basil. It wasn't entirely fair

to him either, to have such a divided heart. One's emotional attachments could be both a bane and a blessing to one's heart. Her bedroom was a constant reminder of her late husband. Elegant, well-crafted furniture with intricate carvings in the wood, a gold and ivory chair near windows dressed in long ivory net curtains. They had stayed here on their honeymoon back in 1913. She had a fond memory of Daniel playing Frank Croxton's "Road to Mandalay" on the old gramophone that still sat in the corner, and the two of them dancing, if not a bit awkwardly, along the shiny wooden floor.

She needed to go for a walk and clear her head.

"Shall I take you out today?" She scrubbed Boss behind the ears.

Lizzie and Scout usually took the pup out for his morning walk, a task Ginger had taken full responsibility for before moving to London. She needed to assuage her guilty feelings in more than one area it seemed.

First things, first. Nature called!

Miss Hanson was just exiting the lavatory. Her eyes drooped, and shadows had made a home under them. Poor thing was finding it hard to sleep lately. Her gaze was downward, and she nearly ran into Ginger on her way back to her bedroom.

"Oh, excuse me, Lady Gold!" Her voice was tinged with weariness. "I feel I'm wearing a path to the loo these days!" She rubbed her protruding belly. "I pity women who are still using chamber pots."

"It's quite all right, Miss Hanson. I do hope you can get some rest now."

"You and me both."

Back in her bedroom, Ginger opened the doors to her wardrobe. The bright May day warranted a happy blue frock with a white sailor collar trimmed in gold ribbon. It had round bone buttons down the front beyond the horizontal band that fit around the hips. A sheer netting hung open over the blue rayon skirt that landed mid-calf. Even though the outfit would be hidden under her spring jacket, one never knew what might happen in one's day, and Ginger had learned to be prepared for anything. She finished up with light makeup and a matching blue sea-themed cloche hat.

"That should do, Bossy. Let's see if we can scrounge up some breakfast before we go."

Ginger had risen earlier than she usually did, but Mrs. Beasley, the cook, rose even earlier. Ginger was heartened by the smell of fresh bread.

"Good morning, Mrs. Beasley," she said brightly.

Mrs. Beasley jumped back from the stove where bacon sizzled in hot grease. "Oh, madam," she said with a puffy hand to her chest. "You startled me. Good morning."

"I'm sorry about that," Ginger said sincerely. "It smells heavenly in here!"

"I'll quickly scramble up some eggs, madam." She turned to her assistant, Grace. "Get Lady Gold some tea."

The young maid bobbed and immediately filled a

kettle at the sink. Scout scampered down the stairs from the attic and almost fell into the room. "Is Boss here, yet?"

Ginger chuckled. "He is and must be let outside at once, though I'll do the morning walk myself today."

Scout's young eyes looked briefly disappointed, but Boss' affections quickly put the smile back on his face. They disappeared into the back garden, and Ginger left for the morning room. French windows overlooked the garden veranda. Ginger opened them, allowing the sweet scent of the spring flora to filter in.

Pippins presented the morning edition of an American paper Ginger subscribed to. It was a day late, but Ginger found it helped her to keep track of what was going on in America—her second home.

"Thank you, dear Pips."

Pippins, a genial septuagenarian had been employed by the Hartigan family for years, and Ginger considered him part of the family. His cornflower-blue eyes relayed his affection for Ginger, which she returned in huge measure. Now that her father was gone, Pips' presence was a comfort.

"So, what's going on in the world today, Pips?"

"It's a hundred and eight degrees in the state of Oregon," Pippins said. "A place called Blitzen."

"Oh mercy," Ginger said. "In May?" She smirked at her butler. "I suppose when you name your town 'lightning' it's bound to get hot."

Pippins ducked his chin allowing for a small smile

at her German language joke. "We can be thankful for our tolerable spring here in jolly old London," he said.

Lizzie, a young maid with short dark hair tucked under a maid's cap, entered with the tea. "You're up early this morning, madam."

"I always wake earlier when the sun is out. Can't take sunshine for granted around here."

Lizzie poured for Ginger and nodded. "That's the truth, madam."

Scout returned with Boss in tow. "His business is done, missus."

"Great. By the way, Scout, how have your lessons been going?"

Scout wrinkled his small nose. "My fingers is crampin' wiv all the writin', and I 'specially dun't like numbers."

"You're just not used to it yet," Ginger encouraged. "The better you get at something, the more you'll like it."

"If you say so, missus. I gotta go 'n' feed Goldmine now."

"Of course."

The rest of Ginger's breakfast arrived. Haley hadn't appeared, and Ginger had no one to talk to. She finished quickly, and before long, she had Boss on a leash and was walking him toward Kensington Gardens, only a short stroll across Kensington Road. Several princesses, a couple of princes, and a marchioness were among the current occupants, though one would be hard-pressed to ever spot one of them in the park.

Ginger made a turn down Flower Walk toward the Albert Memorial. Songbirds chirped from their perches in birch and sweet chestnut trees. Rose gardens burst brightly into bloom. With such beauty as this, Ginger couldn't help but feel a deep sense of contentment. All was well with the world.

Until it wasn't.

Boss alerted Ginger to trouble with sharp barks. Instead of his middling interest in the foliage, taking moments to mark one or two in the way dogs do, he tugged on his leash, leading Ginger to one particular bush. Ginger spotted a lady's boot, and her pulse raced. She ran to the object until the owner was in view. A woman lay facedown on the dew-covered grass. Partially clothed, it looked like the victim had been attacked. She was hatless, and her hair hung in loose, matted waves down her back.

Ginger removed her glove and pressed two fingers to the woman's neck. Her skin was blue and cold. The woman was dead. Knowing not to move the body, Ginger lifted it gently, just to get a view of the face. She let out an audible gasp.

The body belonged to Emelia Reed.

CHAPTER SIX

Oh, mercy.

Foam? Vomit? A white substance traced Emelia's blue lips. The sleeves of her frock were torn, and the hem was pushed up over her knees. She was underdressed for the season, but Ginger could see no sign of a discarded coat or hat.

No obvious puncture wounds or blood, but her forearms showed bruising. Distinctive marks, like thumbprints. The fingers of Emelia's right hand was closed in a fist, and Ginger pried them open, removing the small item. A hair clip.

Ginger thought her throat would close up. A Lucy and Edgardo story button pin. The rare pin that had previously belonged to Dorothy West's grandmother? How was Ginger's shop assistant involved?

Boss whined at her feet.

"I know, Boss. This is terrible." However Emelia

Reed had died, it was clear it wasn't natural or accidental.

Ginger ran back to the path and called for help. Soon she had the attention of a stocky police officer on foot patrol.

"Constable! Come quickly. Please. A woman has been killed."

Ginger had confirmed the identity of the body to the constable, instructing him to talk to someone other than Basil when he called the Yard. Still, Basil was intuitive, a trait that made him good at his job, and it wouldn't take much to set his nose on the scent that something was up.

Ginger sighed when she spotted the large, lumbering body of Superintendent Morris pad toward her. She'd had her run-ins with the obstinate man in the past.

"Why am I not surprised to see you here, Lady Gold?" he bellowed.

"I was simply out walking my dog, Superintendent," Ginger stated, safely tucking Boss under her arm. She didn't want one of the officers to accidentally step on the small animal.

"And you've confirmed the identity, I understand." He frowned as he took in the scantily dressed body lying face down.

"I only lifted the body slightly to look at the face," Ginger said defensively. "You can imagine my shock."

A familiar voice called out: female and American. "Ginger?"

LEE STRAUSS

"Miss Higgins!" The sight of Haley approaching flooded Ginger with relief. "Are you the acting medical examiner?"

"Dr. Wood has a bad case of indigestion, so he sent me on ahead." Haley, wearing her standard no-nonsense tweed suit and low-heel Oxfords approached the body with a doctor's bag in hand. Ginger bent down beside her. "It's Emelia Reed."

Haley's brown eyes flashed in disbelief.

"May I move the body, Superintendent?" Haley asked stiffly. She also wasn't a fan of the blustering, over-sized man.

Morris lifted a beefy palm. "One moment, Miss Higgins. Let's not be hasty. When did you say Dr. Wood was coming?"

"Shortly."

"We'll wait for *him* then." He muttered something about females doing a man's job. Ginger pinched her lips tight to keep from letting him have it.

Pushed to the side, Ginger and Haley watched as the gruff superintendent examined the scene. "This bloody sunshine has dried the turf. Not one bloody footprint." He motioned to a constable. "Anything?"

The constable shook his head. "We've searched the area, sir. Nothing out of the ordinary."

"Did anyone hear or see anything? Early morning dog-walkers?"

The constable tilted his head toward Ginger. "Just this lady, sir."

"Right, right, right." Superintendent Morris focused

in on Ginger like a bull on a red cape. He stomped over and demanded, "Tell me everything that happened."

"As I mentioned before, I was simply out walking my dog." She stroked the animal's head. "It was Boss who alerted me."

Morris' thick brow buckled. "Your boss alerted you? I wasn't aware you were in someone's employ."

"Boss is my dog."

Morris snorted. "That'd be the day when a mutt was the boss of me."

"He's not a *mutt*. He's a Boston terrier." Ginger was losing patience with the superintendent's abrasive manner and his apparent purposeful ignorance.

Morris dismissed her comment with a wave of his beefy hand. "Then what happened?"

Before Ginger could answer, Dr. Wood arrived. His brow was damp with perspiration, and his skin was pale. He indeed looked like he was suffering from some ailment.

"Miss Higgins?" he said. "What have you learned?"

"Nothing so far, sir. Superintendent Morris refused to give me access to the body."

Dr. Wood sent Morris a withering look. "Why on earth not?"

Morris stammered. "She's not a doctor!"

"Miss Higgins is my summer intern and is here on my authority."

Haley cast a wry glance Ginger's way and Ginger bit the inside of her lip. She liked Dr. Wood. He took no guff from the superintendent.

Morris wrinkled his face and turned back to Ginger. "Continue, madam."

Please.

Ginger had no choice but to ignore the superintendent's rudeness. "First, I saw her boot. It extended just beyond the bush. When I went over to investigate, I discovered the body. I first checked for a pulse and on finding none, I immediately returned to the path in search of assistance, and that constable," Ginger nodded to the stocky foot officer, "responded to my calls for help."

The superintendent raised a bushy brow. "You *immediately* called for help?"

"Well, I took a peek at the face, first. I didn't move the body, just lifted it slightly. That's when I recognized Mrs. Reed."

Morris sniffed. "That's all for now. You may go."

"May I?" Ginger asked impertinently. Kensington Gardens was a public park, and she would go when it very well pleased her!

"Yes, Lady Gold," Morris responded, not catching Ginger's sarcasm. "And it goes without saying that you are to stay out of the investigation!"

"Of course," Ginger said, Dorothy West's hair clip pressed firmly in her hand.

"Dr. Wood," Morris bellowed. "Cause of death?"

"I'm afraid that's undetermined," Dr. Wood said. "We need to take the body to the mortuary for a postmortem."

"What about time of death, then?" Morris asked

impatiently.

"Rigor has yet to set in," Haley answered in Dr. Wood's stead. "I'd say two to three hours ago."

Morris snorted and stared at Dr. Wood.

Dr. Wood held his stomach, distinctly uncomfortable with whatever was going on inside there. "I concur with Miss Higgins. The postmortem may narrow that window." Dr. Wood walked away without saying another word.

A commotion stirred up with the arrival of the ambulance attendants.

"Emelia?"

Ginger's chest caved. "Basil!" She handed Boss to Haley and ran to him.

His eyes flickered wildly as he tried to see past her. "Is it true? Is it Emelia?"

Ginger's mouth dropped open. *Dear God, am I to be the one to announce that his estranged wife is dead?*

He didn't wait for her to answer but dodged past her to where Emelia's body lay, now face turned to the sky.

"No, Emelia! No, no, no!" Basil skidded to his knees and leaned over Emelia Reed's dead, half-dressed form. His face paled to a ghostly white as the muscles in his jaw twitched, and his lips worked in vain to check his emotions. He pinched his eyes tight as his hand went to his face and his heavy shoulders trembled. Try as he might, the stalwart man couldn't keep a sob from escaping.

Ginger watched in stunned silence.

CHAPTER SEVEN

oldmine, Ginger's gorgeous new horse, was an Akhal-Teke. Originally from Turkmenistan, the rare breed was known for its silky hair. Goldmine's golden mane shone brilliantly in the mid-morning sun.

The weather was perfect for a ride through Hyde Park. The air smelled sweet and fresh, and the warmth of the sun's rays soothed the tension in Ginger's face. Goldmine carried Ginger as if she were royalty—the gelding's gait smooth and confident. The comforting clip-clop of his shoes on the path created a lovely melody. The sheen of Goldmine's spectacular coat caught the eye of every passer-by. Ginger nodded proudly. With a straw cloche hat and a pale yellow riding blazer, she wore her new riding skirt, *astride*.

Ginger had been rapturous to leave her side-saddle in Boston. How liberating to ride like a man, well-balanced and one with the horse. No more twisted hips and fear of being tossed about like a bag of potatoes. Ginger's boldness elicited the occasional glare of disapproval from both men and women alike, but she wouldn't let their old-fashioned beliefs deter her. Suffrage had brought women more than just the vote.

She should be deliriously happy, but instead, she felt like a hollowed-out shell. The image of Basil weeping for his wife replayed in her mind like a silent film. All this time he'd been courting Ginger—he'd only just yesterday declared his love for her! —he was still in love with Emelia.

Hypocrite!

Wasn't she guilty of the same thing with Daniel?

When Basil had been recovering from his gunshot wound in the hospital, Ginger had witnessed Emelia with him moments before she left his room in tears. Ginger had assumed—based on the fact that Emelia disappeared and Basil now called on Ginger—that Basil had been the one to send Emelia away, that he'd finally had enough of her philandering ways. But maybe, Emelia had left Basil, the tears pouring from her eyes because once again, she had broken his heart?

When Ginger approached the park, she let the gelding loose with a click of her tongue and a snap of the reins. Bending low, boots firmly in the stirrups, her thighs pinching the saddle, she forced her mind to empty, to become one with the horse. Goldmine's gallop was so smooth that Ginger felt as if she were flying with the wind. For those few blessed moments, she was free from the tangled, strangling pain in her heart. For two minutes, she forgot about Basil Reed.

By the time Ginger got back to the stable at Hartigan House, she felt better. She was a strong woman, master of her emotions. She would be fine.

"Missus!" Scout shouted on seeing her. "How'd Goldmine do?"

"Marvelous," Ginger said as she dismounted. "Did you want to go for a ride?"

Scout's chin fell, and he shuffled backward shyly. "Na, I couldn't."

"Why not? You were the one to name him after all."

Scout's head bobbed up with his big smile fixed in place. "I did, dinn't I? But, missus, I dunno 'ow to ride. I mean, I's fine with 'orses from the ground, but that's way up there!"

Ginger tried not to smile. She knew her charge couldn't ride. Learning how was, mostly, a privilege held by the upper classes. "It's *horse*, Scout. You must learn to pronounce the H."

"Yes, missus," Scout said with an exasperated breath. "*Horse.*"

"How about I teach you? I won't let go of the reins. I'll just lead you in the garden behind the garage."

"Yer won't let go?"

"I promise."

Ginger hoisted Scout onto Goldmine and adjusted the stirrups to fit his short legs. "Just hold onto the saddle," she instructed, unnecessarily. Scout's small knuckles grew white as he held on for dear life.

42

"Go slow!"

"I will," Ginger said taking Goldmine forward a few steps. "The trick to riding is to relax. A horse can feel if its rider is nervous, and it makes them nervous."

"It ain't so easy, missus. I dun't wanna fall."

"You'll catch on, Scout. I have faith in you."

After a short trip around the garage and back, Scout had learned to relax a little.

"See, that wasn't so bad," Ginger said.

"It was great, missus! I love Goldmine so much!"

Ginger chuckled. "He loves you too. Now, I'll help you down, and you can cool Goldmine off."

Scout led Goldmine into his stall. Ginger instructed him on how to remove the saddle—on the heavy side for a small lad, but he managed. "You already know how to remove the bit and how to brush him down."

"I do, missus."

Ginger was about to leave when she remembered something else. "I spoke to Reverend Hill, Scout. He said he'd like to talk to you about Marvin."

Scout's countenance darkened. "Oh, I dun't fink so, missus."

"Why not? I thought you and he were friends."

"It's not Reverend 'ill, just the church 'all. Reminds me of when I always was 'ungry. I ain't been 'ungry since coming to 'artigan 'ouse."

If Ginger's heartstrings hadn't been pulled by Scout's confession, she would've insisted he repeat himself and pick up all the H's. Instead, she held onto her emotion and spoke softly. "Well, you won't be hungry when you go there this time, and you won't be staying for long, just for a visit. I thought it might help you to have a man to talk to."

"I talk to Mr. Pippins and Mr. Clement."

"Of course. I meant a man who knows Marvin. I could invite him to come to see you here."

"I suppose, dat would be all right."

"Good. I'll arrange a meeting."

Ginger headed to the back entrance at Hartigan House with her spirits much lifted. Goldmine and Scout Elliot were mood elixirs.

Pippins waited for her by the door. "Is everything all right, Pips?"

"You have a visitor waiting in the sitting room."

A giant pit instantly formed in Ginger's stomach. "Is it Chief Inspector Reed?"

Pippins tucked his chin. "It is, madam."

CHAPTER EIGHT

*B*asil Reed, the chief inspector of the criminal investigative division at Scotland Yard, was always so resolute, principled, controlled, and unflinching. He'd be a master at poker if he played the game, an expert at concealing his emotions at will —but not today. The man who stood before her in his crumpled suit looked weak and broken. His normally handsome face was etched with raw emotion. His hazel eyes, dark with sadness, were tired and rimmed with red.

Basil Reed's grief was palpable and profound, washing over Ginger in waves. Her knees trembled, and she eased slowly into her chair.

"Basil, I'm so sorry—"

"No. It is I who must apologize." Basil swallowed hard and sat in the chair next to her. Bending toward

her, he anchored his elbows onto his knees. "I'm sorry
you had to see that—see me like that."

"You've suffered a great shock."

"Yes. Quite. But for you, when we—"

"We what, Basil?" Ginger said, then shook her head.
"No, forget that. Your wife is dead, and you need time
to mourn. I can grant you that."

Ginger hated the bitterness that sprinkled
her words.

"Ginger," Basil said. Longing for *something* flashed
behind his eyes. Understanding? Forgiveness?

"It's okay," Ginger said with a long sigh. "You loved
Emelia. She was your wife."

"Someone killed her, Ginger, and I need to find
out who."

Ginger understood that. If Daniel's life had been
taken in such a manner, she wouldn't have rested until
the culprit was brought to justice.

"I'm sure it's now Scotland Yard's top priority,"
Ginger said.

"Morris took me off the case. He's forced me to
take leave."

For once Ginger and Morris agreed on something.

"It's for the best, Basil. You're clearly too close to it.
Too emotionally involved."

Basil flinched at the word *emotionally*.

"I think we should have some tea," Ginger said.
"Would you like some tea?"

Basil nodded mutely.

Ginger rang the bell for the kitchen, and shortly afterwards, Grace entered the sitting room. "Madam?"

"We would like some tea."

Grace bobbed. "Yes, madam. Right away."

Basil reached for Ginger's hand, but she pretended she didn't see it and shifted in her seat. She didn't know where she stood anymore with Basil's affection. Once again, she felt like a distant second runner-up.

And she felt petty for feeling that way. She stood and moved to the fireplace, busying herself by poking at the flames. Above the mantel was an empty spot, the bricks a lighter shade of brown where *The Mermaid* had hung for almost two decades.

Why had she given it away?

Thankfully, Grace returned swiftly with the tea. She set it on the coffee table between Ginger and Basil's chairs and poured two cups.

"Thank you, Grace," Ginger said. "That's all for now."

Silence stretched between Ginger and Basil as they each took their first sip.

"I'm going to find her killer," Basil said. His voice was stronger now, edged with anger and determination.

"Are you sure that's wise?" Ginger asked gently.

"I'm not going to leave it to that moron, Morris."

Ginger held in her surprise. Never once in the nine months Ginger had known Basil had he spoken harshly and with disrespect about his superior officer. She couldn't correct him, though, since she agreed with his assessment.

"I want you to help me, Ginger," Basil said earnestly. "You and I, we make a good investigative team."

Ginger lifted her teacup to her mouth, hoping to hide the conflicting emotions she felt at Basil's request. They made a good *investigative* team. Were they now relegated back to business partners? Was she just to forget the way he'd often kissed her? Forget that they had declared love to each other?

Perhaps it was for the best. Basil was in no position to commit to another romance when his heart was still obviously attached to Emelia. And if the killer weren't caught, he never would be.

"Okay," she said quietly. "I'll help you."

Basil held her gaze. "Thank you."

"If you'll excuse me," Ginger said while rising, "I need to change out of my riding clothes."

Basil's eyes moved from Ginger's face, registering her less-than-conventional clothing as if for the first time. "Yes, of course." He collapsed like a rag doll in his chair. "I'll wait here."

Upstairs, Ginger hurried to remove her clothing, taking a few minutes to clean up. Her mind raced for what to wear. She gravitated to her darker colors, not quite black, but a step back from spring pastel. It seemed inappropriate to dress for the living at the moment.

And a suit, rather than a dress. Not quite as conventional as the tweed outfits Haley preferred, but sensible.

She had taken off her emerald ring before riding Goldmine, a piece she had started wearing after she stopped wearing her wedding ring. A piece of her wanted to dig the diamond out of her bedside table, but she resisted and decided to go ringless instead. Her eye landed on the distinctive hair clip she'd removed from Emelia's cold grip. Was it Dorothy's? How then did Emelia have it? And what, other than customer and sales clerk, had been their relationship? Ginger's heart squeezed with worry for her employee. She was fond of Dorothy and hoped desperately that she hadn't got herself into some kind of trouble.

The kind that could find her dead in a park.

There was the other issue of her own, now undeniable, misdemeanor. Tampering with the scene of a crime, not to mention withholding evidence from the police.

Should she tell Basil?

No, she'd wait until after she had a chance to talk to Dorothy herself.

When Ginger returned to the sitting room, Basil looked like he hadn't moved an inch. Ginger wondered if he'd fallen asleep, but he shifted when he heard her come in.

"What's our first move?" Ginger asked without preamble.

CHAPTER NINE

Kensington Palace *did* look like a place where vampires might dwell. The flash of good weather Londoners had enjoyed earlier had been whipped out like a tablecloth from under a full-course meal. A cloud bank, so dark that it was hard to tell the time of day, had rolled in. Fog simmered through the park like a sheet of cotton, and Ginger swore she saw a bat fly overhead. Rain began to dance on her open umbrella.

Basil opened his black umbrella and held it over-head. "Take me along the exact route you took this morning."

They'd done this once already, before scouring the rest of the park for anything that might lead to the killer. The moody weather didn't help with visibility, and so far they had found nothing unusual. Ginger headed back to the Flower Walk.

"I entered the park there and turned onto the path here." Going over the scene of the crime more than once was standard detecting procedure, but Ginger worried that Basil's drive to work the case was obsessive rather than deductive.

"Boss started barking when I reached this point, and from here I could see Emelia's boot."

Basil zigzagged his way to the place the body had been found, eyes to the ground. Ginger followed. The indentation of Emelia's body was still evident.

"Ginger, would you mind terribly to . . ." Basil motioned limply, and Ginger gasped slightly at what she perceived to be his request.

"You want to act it out?"

"It could be helpful."

"But we don't know how she died?"

"This could lead to an answer." Basil shook his head. "No, you're right. I shouldn't have asked this of you."

Ginger inhaled deeply. "I'll do it."

"No, it's—"

"Basil, I said I'd help."

"Right." Basil's discomfort was apparent in the way he failed to meet her eyes. "She was here, with someone."

"I'll be her," Ginger said. "And you be—the killer." They didn't know for sure if the killer was male or female.

Ginger closed her umbrella and dropped it on the ground. Basil did the same. "Grab my arms," she said. "There was bruising on her forearms."

Basil took a tentative step forward and took her arms.

"That's not right," Ginger said. She stepped back and removed her coat. "She wasn't wearing a jacket. The bruising happened because the killer had her by her bare arms."

The rain immediately dampened her blouse. Ginger pushed up her sleeves and held out her arms. Basil took them, gripped them tightly. The move forced them to stand close, closer than they had at any moment since Emelia's death. Ginger felt the heat of Basil's palms on her skin, his hot breath on her cheek. Her heart raced, and had this been any other day, any other moment, it would've been romantic. As it was, it was horribly awkward.

Ginger stared at Basil's grip. "It's wrong.""

"What do you mean?"

"The thumbprint was on the underside."

Basil studied the position of his thumbs. "He held her from behind."

Ginger turned around, and Basil gripped Ginger's arms. "But what did he do to her?" Basil said. "How did he kill her?"

"She ended up facedown on the lawn," Ginger said. "Perhaps he pushed her." Ginger dropped to the ground.

"You don't have to do that," Basil said. "It's wet."

"It might help." Ginger lay face down in the exact position Emelia had been when she found her.

"Ginger," Basil's voice cracked.

"I don't think she died here," Ginger said, ignoring the plea in Basil's voice. She pushed herself off the ground, and Basil helped her to her feet. He picked up Ginger's coat and held it open for her.

"Why do you think that," Basil said as Ginger slipped her coat on over her damp frock.

"I think she struggled. It would explain the defensive wounds and her torn clothing. Why wasn't she wearing a coat? It looked to me like she had vomited, yet there's no sign of sick anywhere here."

"If that's the case, we need to find the scene of the crime," Basil said soberly. "I saw Miss Higgins with . . . the body . . . didn't I?"

"Yes. She was there along with Dr. Wood from University College Hospital."

Basil nodded. "Let's go and talk to her. Maybe they've found something."

CHAPTER TEN

*G*inger didn't deem Basil fit to drive, so insisted on their taking the Crossley. She could've called for a taxicab, but that would've wasted time, plus, she didn't want a stranger to overhear their conversation, and Ginger definitely had questions. Uncharacteristically, Basil relented with little resistance.

The shortest route was West Carriage Drive through Kensington Gardens that cut through Hyde Park, and even that took nearly half an hour. The sun had arrived with the dawn along with women pushing baby prams, couples walking hand in hand, elderly folk casually feeding bread to the ducks on the Serpentine. For so many Londoners and tourists, it was just another ordinary day. None were even aware that a woman had lost her life in a most horrible way and had been left in this popular green space just that morning.

The way Basil stared morosely out of his window with brows furrowed and deepening frown lines had Ginger wondering if he was thinking the same thing.

She waited until safely past Marble Arch on Great Cumberland Place before asking preliminary questions. She kept her eyes straight ahead and *not* on Basil.

"Do you have any idea where Emelia was living after she left you?"

"She has a flat in Campden Hill."

"Nice area." Campden Hill was an affluent area between Notting Hill, Kensington, and Holland Park. She and Emelia were practically neighbors. Ginger was surprised she hadn't run into Emelia Reed at Kensington Gardens before. It made her wonder if Basil had dropped in at Hartigan House *after* calling in at Emelia's. "Does she have friends?"

"I presume so. None that we share, any longer."

"Did she take frequent walks in the park?"

Basil sighed heavily. "I really don't know. Perhaps. She was close enough, I suppose."

Traffic was heavy along Marylebone Road through The Regent's Park, and Ginger thought that traveling on the underground might be the way of the future for her, at least, if she were in a hurry like today. It would be hard to give up the comfort and independence of the Crossley, though, but she'd keep an open mind.

Like the London School of Medicine for Women, the mortuary at University College Hospital was in the cellar but brightened with white paint and electric lights.

"Ginger," Haley said. Her eyes moved to Basil and back with a questioning look. "What are you doing here?"

"Basil and I were told to keep our noses out of this case," Ginger said, "but really, Haley, did you think that was at all possible?"

Haley's lips twitched. "Knowing you, no."

Ginger followed Basil's quiet gaze to the white sheet covering his wife's body on the ceramic slab.

"Inspector Reed," Haley said, "I'm sorry for your loss."

Ginger read the message behind her friend's eyes. She was sorry a woman had died but didn't like how Basil was treating Ginger now.

Basil just said, "Thank you."

Haley pinched the edges of the sheet near the head. "Are you sure you're up to this?"

"Yes. I'll be fine," he added. "It was just the initial shock . . ."

"Have you and Dr. Wood determined cause of death?" Ginger asked.

"Well," Haley's dark eyes flickered from Ginger to Basil and back. "Take a look at this." Haley pulled the sheet back revealing Emelia's ghostly white face.

The muscles in Basil's face tightened, his lips forming a knot, but he didn't falter. "What are we looking for?"

Haley gently turned Emelia's head to expose the right side of her neck, revealing two red dots like incisor marks.

"She was bitten?" Basil asked, incredulously.

Ginger swallowed as she thought about Felicia's fanciful vampire notion. Haley saved her from embarrassing herself.

"It looks like a snake bite."

Ginger wondered how she had missed this earlier, but then again, Emelia's hair was down, and Ginger had been careful not to disturb the body.

"She appears to have vomited which supports snake venom poisoning. We'll know more after the postmortem."

"When will that be?" Basil asked.

"In the next couple of days."

"Are there venomous snakes in England?" Ginger thought not, but one couldn't know everything.

"Just the adder," Basil said. "It only bites if it feels threatened, and almost always the bite is on a limb, not the neck. It can be quite deadly if not treated immediately."

So, someone held a snake, an adder, likely, to Emelia's neck. Ginger's mouth grew sour. How macabre. An act of passion, surely. Who hated Emelia Reed that much?

Ginger tapped her forearms. "I saw bruising."

Haley nodded and reached under the sheet to extract one arm. "She was held tightly by someone with considerable strength. A man or a strong woman."

Basil swallowed hard. "Had she been, er, compromised?"

"There's no evidence of . . . force," Haley answered delicately.

"Dr. Wood and I began to question time of death. The cooler temperatures of night should slow the process of rigor, especially since she was without a hat or jacket.

"But," Ginger prompted.

"We thought she was still in primary flaccidity—the stage before rigor mortis, but on further examination of the body, it appears she's already gone through rigor. Decomposition has set in."

"What does that mean about the time of death?" Ginger asked.

"It means she was killed last night, not this morning."

Basil let out a frustrated sigh, and Ginger didn't blame him. It meant the killer had had hours to get away.

"There's something else," Haley said. "I initially thought her dress had been torn, shortening the hem, but . . ." She picked up an item on one of the counters and held it up. "The hemline is sewn perfectly."

Haley held it up to her body to demonstrate how short it was, the hemline falling to just above the knee.

"The décolletage is rather low," Ginger muttered.

Haley folded the costume, readying it for evidence. "Her stockings were twisted and torn."

Ginger didn't want to speak aloud what that could mean. "Can you tell if she'd been moved?" she asked. "Was she killed somewhere other than the park?"

"I believe she was dumped there," Haley said. When Basil blanched, she corrected herself. "*Deposited*, there."

"What makes you think that?" Basil asked stoically.

"Lividity. The pooling of the blood was more concentrated on the left side. If she had died in the position she was found, flat, then lividity should be evenly distributed. She died on her side, bite mark up."

"Is it possible that Emelia had been participating in some kind of burlesque routine?" Ginger asked. She glanced apologetically at Basil. It was a horrible question and she hated asking it.

"I'm afraid so," Haley said. "Superintendent Morris was here earlier and apparently one of his constables at the scene recognized her from a town club."

"Which one?" Basil asked.

"Unfortunately, the constable couldn't remember," Haley said. "Apparently, he frequents several."

Ginger leaned closer to the body and breathed in. "French perfume."

Basil cleared his throat, and Ginger avoided his eyes. You didn't have to be a detective to deduce that Emelia had most likely been selling favors. But what kind of favors? No one was certain.

CHAPTER ELEVEN

*G*inger used the mortuary telephone book to look up the addresses of the numerous burlesque clubs in the city. The task might take longer than they thought it would.

"I've written them down in geographical sequence. There's one not far from here in Kings Cross. The North Star."

"We should start with the one closest to Kensington Gardens," Basil said.

"Of course." It was the small things that broadcast Basil's experience and her lack of it. Although someone could've driven Emelia to the park, she supposed. She rewrote the list starting with the club in Notting Hill.

A heavy, awkward silence rested between them in the Crossley, just like it had when Emelia had first re-entered Basil's life after a two-year absence. Ginger and Basil had only been friendly at the time, but if they were honest, their encounters bordered on flirtatious and their relationship had been moving toward something more. Emelia was responsible for the barrier again, her ability to cripple whatever lay between Ginger and Basil just as effective in her death as in her life. Ginger wondered if she and Basil would ever be rid of her essence.

Ginger parked in front of the run-down Notting Hill establishment. Lights that would shine brightly in the night, and the corresponding energy of jazz music that would filter out of the door each time it opened were now dark, quiet, and empty.

"I didn't consider it might not be open," Basil said. "But of course, a proprietor like this doesn't hold to normal business hours."

"There might still be someone inside," Ginger said, though she didn't hold out much hope.

"We're here anyway," Basil said, wearily. "It wouldn't hurt to take a look around."

The brick exterior of the club had no windows, and the door needed paint. Litter tucked into the base of the cement foundation. A stench of urine reached Ginger's nose. Ginger could imagine the clientele this establishment attracted, and she couldn't believe Emelia would become entwined with such a place. At least, Ginger certainly hoped not.

Knocking on the front entrance produced no response.

"Maybe the back door," Ginger suggested.

There was a narrow space between the club and the next building, and with each step closer to the alley the litter mounds grew larger and the stench increased.

Basil rapped his knuckles on the wooden door.

It appeared that there would be no answer, and they had already turned to go when the door opened. A diminutive man in loose-fitting clothing spoke gruffly. "Whatcha want?"

Basil produced his identification card. "I'm Chief Inspector Reed of Scotland Yard. Who might you be?"

"Name's Benson. Co-owner of this establishment."

Basil held out a photograph to the man. Ginger glimpsed the image of Emelia, alive and smiling, eyes sparkling with joy. The picture had been cut down the middle. Ginger recognized Basil's shoulder and jawline, tucked in close.

"Have you seen this woman, Mr. Benson?" Basil asked.

Benson studied the photo and shook his head.

"Never seen her. I already told this to the other guy. "

Basil frowned. "What other guy?"

"Some bigwig. Morris, I think he said his name was. He didn't have a photograph, but he was asking after a brunette."

"I see. Well, thank you for your time, Mr. Benson," Basil said.

Back in the Crossley Basil muttered, "Morris is already ahead of us."

"Let's start from the other end, then," Ginger said. "We'll meet in the middle."

"He can't know we're investigating. If you remember, he pulled me off the case, and you are on his blacklist."

"We'll make sure to watch out for him," Ginger said with a sigh.

Basil stared morosely out of the window. "Let's do as you suggested, head to the North Star."

IN STARK CONTRAST, the North Star had newly painted wooden window frames and a large professionally printed sign surrounded by extinguished light bulbs. Only the typical London smells of motorcar exhaust and horse manure assaulted Ginger's nose. It was classier than the last one, which reflected the status of the clientele that would frequent it, (even though each member of the gentry would steadfastly deny ever having crossed the threshold.)

Basil knocked on the door, and this time it opened.

"Yeah?" The man said suspiciously. He barely gave Ginger a cursory glance.

Basil flashed his card. "I'm Chief Inspector Basil Reed. And you are?"

"Conway Sayer, club manager."

Basil held out Emelia's photo. "Do you know this woman?"

The man's expression remained unchanged as he

stared at Emelia's image. "What if I did? Is she in trouble with the law?"

Basil swallowed. "She's dead. Murdered sometime last night."

The man's face softened. "Blimey. I'm sorry to hear it. Destiny was a popular gal."

Ginger exchanged a glance with Basil. *Destiny*? Like the Waterhouse painting.

"Not her real name, I imagine," Mr. Sayer continued. "All the gals here use phony names to protect their privacy."

Basil cleared his throat. "When was the last time you saw, er, Destiny?"

"Last night, during her show. She disappeared right afterwards. Maybe she left with a client."

Basil's mortification radiated off him in hot waves, and Ginger felt herself blush at this revelation. Had Emelia *really* been a *doxy*? What on earth for? Why in heaven's name would she choose this life over a domesticated one with Basil?

"Did she leave any personal items behind?" Basil asked.

"Maybe. The gals do each have a cupboard, but it's up to them to lock it if they want."

"Do you mind if we step inside," Basil said. "I'd like to have a look at . . . Destiny's cupboard."

The man hesitated.

"This is a murder investigation, Mr. Sayer."

The man stepped backward and waved them in.

The walls of the dressing room area were lined with

mirrors, each flanked with big bright bulbs and a chair facing it. Racks of bright costumes included a variety of corsets and underthings, and there were accordion screens with Egyptian print for a modicum of privacy. Behind the door on the wall was a row of cupboards. Mr. Sayer tapped on one. "This was Destiny's. Now if you don't mind, I have work to attend to." The club manager left them alone.

Basil stared at the cupboard door, unmoving.

"Perhaps I should look inside," Ginger said. Basil nodded subtly.

Ginger shifted in front of Basil, attempting to block his view. The last thing he needed was another big shock. She inhaled and slowly opened the door.

A jade-green silk frock was folded neatly inside, along with a pair of white T-strap shoes and a white short-brimmed hat, all items of good quality that would sell at a reasonable price. "Just some clothes," Ginger said, shifting aside. "This must be what she wore when she arrived yesterday." Before she performed her *show*. "Do you want to tag them as evidence?" Ginger added briefly forgetting that Basil was no longer in official authoritative capacity. "No," she added quickly. "I suppose you can't."

"We must," Basil said, surprising her. "There may be evidence among them, and I don't trust Morris to get it right."

Basil always had paper evidence bags tucked in the pockets of his overcoat and he produced three. With gloved hands, Ginger dropped each item in as Basil held the openings wide.

"We'll get Haley to examine these," Ginger said. "She has access to the hospital labs."

Ginger safely deposited the evidence bags in the boot of the motorcar and was about to drive off when a hard knocking of the knuckles on her window startled her.

Superintendent Morris' disgruntled face peered through it. Ginger shot Basil a look—caught!

"Well, well, well," Superintendent Morris sang uncharitably as Ginger rolled her window down. "The two of you investigating when I told you both not to."

"Sir," Basil began.

Superintendent Morris held out a palm. "Save your breath, Mr. Reed."

Mr. Reed?

Superintendent Morris' smirk deepened. "I'll have to ask you to come with me to the station."

"Sir, this was my fault," Basil said. "You can take me in, but let Lady Gold go home."

"Oh, I'm taking you in all right. Please step out of the motorcar."

Ginger's heart thudded like a rabbit's. Her nerves were taut and ready to act. Her mind flashed to a similar encounter with the German patrol in France during the war.

Basil held her gaze for a long second before doing as Superintendent Morris asked. Two constables flanked Basil on either side. This couldn't be a good sign. The next second proved it to be a very, very bad sign.

Superintendent Morris' voice reverberated loudly, and Ginger heard his words as she sat in the motorcar. "Basil Reed, you're under arrest on suspicion of murdering your wife, Emelia Reed."

CHAPTER TWELVE

*G*inger fumed on her way back to the city mortuary. *What an imbecile!* Morris couldn't detect a murderer if the killer punched him on the nose!

Once she had Haley's full attention, she explained her and Basil's findings at the North Star. Ginger gesticulated wildly. "Now, instead of looking for the real killer, Basil, who could actually solve the case, is sitting in a locked jail cell!"

"I agree with you," Haley began, "However, it's true that a large majority of women who die violently, do so at the hands of their own spouse."

"Basil did *not* kill Emelia!"

"Of course he didn't," Haley said wisely. "He's smitten with you."

"You wouldn't know it by how he's acting," Ginger murmured.

"Ginger, honey. Basil's in shock. Even though he was no longer with his wife, no longer loved her, Emelia had been a significant person in his life for some years. It's bound to have an impact on him. He wouldn't be human if it didn't."

Ginger paced the floor, hands on hips.

"Yes, I know you're right, but I'm not so sure he's no longer in love with Emelia."

"Well, it's a moot point now, isn't it?"

Ginger dropped onto a wooden chair. "Oh, I'm a horrible person! A woman *died*. I'm feeling jealous of a *dead* person. My main concern should be to solve this case. For Basil's sake, we have to find out who killed her."

"Agreed," Haley said. "What's in the bags?"

Ginger had plopped the evidence bags on a lab countertop. "Emelia's clothes. We found them at the North Star. Luckily, Morris didn't check the boot of my motorcar." This was further proof of the man's ineptness. Basil wouldn't have failed to have a peek.

Haley hummed. "You've got interference in a police investigation down to a science."

Ginger didn't respond to that comment. "Can you look the items over? Maybe there's a clue hidden in there."

"Off the record?"

"Please."

"I'd only do something like this for you, Ginger."

"You're the best of the best, my friend."

NEXT STOP: Feathers and Flair. There was still the matter of Dorothy's grandmother's hairpin, and Ginger had a few questions for her shop assistant.

"Madame Roux," Ginger said with no preamble. "I need to speak to Dorothy."

"*Je suis désolée*, madame," Ginger's shop manager said, "but Miss West is not here. It is her afternoon off."

Ginger's mind brought up the shop's calendar. It was indeed the afternoon Dorothy didn't come into work. Emma took the floor on these days, leaving her duties as a seamstress for days when both girls were in. Ginger picked up the receiver of the elaborately detailed ivory full-handled telephone, dialed the operator, and asked for Dorothy's parents' number. Unfortunately, the West family didn't have a telephone.

"Drat."

"Is everything all right, madam," Madame Roux inquired.

"I'm afraid not. A client who was helped upstairs by Dorothy yesterday has been murdered."

"*Mon dieu*! Who, madam?"

Ginger paused before relaying her answer. Though she and Basil had kept their blossoming relationship discreet, her staff were privy to its nature.

"Mrs. Reed."

Madame Roux's bejeweled fingers flew to her mouth. "Oh, no. Does Inspector Reed know?"

"Yes." No need to fill Madame Roux in on the fact that Basil now sat in a jail cell at Scotland Yard. "It's imperative that I talk to Dorothy. Mrs. Reed might've said or done something that could shed light on the matter."

Emma approached the two women. "I'm sorry, I didn't mean to overhear. Such dreadful news. If you're looking for Dorothy, she told me that she was going to be volunteering at St. George's Church."

Initially astounded by this tidbit of information, on further reflection, it made sense to Ginger. Dorothy's infatuation with Oliver Hill was apparent.

"Thank you, Emma," Ginger said as she headed for the entrance.

Ginger was so consumed with the case that even *she* noticed her driving was on the erratic side. She hadn't heard so many motorcar horns blasting and tires screeching for some weeks. She nearly ran into the back of a slow-moving horse and cart.

"They need to give motorcars their own lane!"

Ginger heard the frustration in her voice. She was worried about Basil. The whole affair was horrid. She needed answers.

Ginger slowed down as she drew up to the church. She was a refined, disciplined lady, not a blast of wind.

She found Mrs. Davies in the rectory. "Mrs. Davies, I'm looking for Miss Dorothy West. Do you know her?"

"Yes, she's a very nice girl. Attends Sunday service regularly."

"Good. I'm told she might be volunteering here today. It's essential that I speak to her."

"She was helping me to sort through the clothing donations, but she's in the garden now having tea with Reverend Hill."

Having tea with Reverend Hill? It seemed an intimate thing to do for a vicar with his sights on another woman, although, Ginger often shared tea alone with Oliver. She couldn't blame the man for being a good host.

Oliver rose to his feet when he saw her, immediately approached her, and took her gloved hand in his. "Lady Gold, so nice to see you."

"And you, Oliver."

Dorothy's previously happy countenance switched to one of distress. She apparently hadn't expected to see her employer today, and especially not here.

"What brings you this way?" Oliver asked jovially.

"Actually, I need to have a word with Miss West if you don't mind. In private."

"Oh, yes, certainly. I have work to do in my office. I'll ask Mrs. Davies to bring some more tea."

"That's not necessary," Ginger said. "I won't be long."

Ginger sat in the garden chair which had been occupied by Oliver only moments before, and Dorothy's expression grew even grimmer.

"What is it, Lady Gold? Is there a problem at the shop?"

"No. I'm afraid it's much more dire than that."

"Oh, dear. What's wrong?"

"One of our clients has been found murdered."

"How awful! Who was it?"

"Emelia Reed."

Dorothy slumped in her chair, the colour in her cheeks draining to white. "Oh, my! I just talked to her yesterday!"

"I know. That is why I had to find you."

"Well, I don't know what to say."

"What did you talk about at the shop?"

Dorothy gulped, then took a sip of tea. If Ginger hadn't known the girl better, she would've guessed that she was about to tell a lie.

"It was a perfectly normal interaction," Dorothy finally said. "She bought a Lanvin."

From her handbag, Ginger removed the story button pin imprinted with the distinctive relief of young lovers. "This was in her fist."

Dorothy looked ill. "It's very much like mine."

"Is it yours?"

"It can't be. I had it in the pocket of my cardigan." Dorothy glanced down. "This cardigan in fact!" She rummaged through the pockets. "It's gone."

"It's important you think back, Dorothy. Tell me everything that happened from the moment she walked into Feathers & Flair to the moment she left.

"I didn't see her enter, so I can't vouch for what she did on the ground floor, but I noticed her immediately as she topped the steps. She always carries herself with such grace and charm. Oh, milady, I'm so sorry to go on about her like that with you and the inspector—"

"It's quite all right," Ginger said, ignoring the cool prickles that ran up her spine. "Continue."

"She asked about how we got our factory dresses, and if anyone bought such a thing," Dorothy hurried to add, "I reassured her that the upper-class lady was very interested in the convenience, and even the price."

"Okay, what else?"

"She took an interest in the Jeanne Lanvin factory line, one of which she later purchased. Then you came upstairs."

"I remember. That was when this clip fell out of your hair."

"Yes. And I put it in this pocket." She patted the pocket on the right-hand side of her cardigan.

"Then I left . . ." Ginger prompted.

"Shortly after that, Mrs. Reed knocked down the rack with the scarves. She helped me to right it."

"Have you ever been to the North Star club?"

Dorothy looked aghast. "No! Never. How could you ask such a thing?"

"I didn't mean to offend you, Dorothy, but it's necessary that I ask certain questions. Did you find yourself in the company of Mrs. Reed anywhere else?"

"No, madam. I only knew who she was because she attended the open house gala at Feathers & Flair."

With Basil.

"Is there anything else, madam?"

"That'll be all for now, Dorothy. I'll let Reverend Hill know that I'm leaving."

She met Oliver in the doorway. Apparently, he was

waiting for them to finish. "Is everything all right?" Oliver asked.

Ginger filled him in on the murder. Oliver expressed his sympathies and hurried back to Dorothy. She was dabbing her tears with a handkerchief as he put his hand on her shoulder to console her.

$\mathcal{B}$asil was being held at the police station near the Old Bailey.

Ginger walked inside the stone building, tall and poised, as if she had every reason in the world to be there and spoke to the constable on duty.

"I would like to visit Mr. Reed."

"And your name, madam?"

"Lady Gold."

"Are you a relative?" The man regarded her suspiciously. "

"No. I'm a friend."

He pushed a clipboard across the counter. "Fill this in, please."

Ginger quickly filled in the paperwork and signed the visitors' register. She caught the constable's eye when she had finished.

"Come with me, madam."

Ginger followed the constable down a narrow passageway, ignoring his fellow service officers as they unabashedly looked on.

There were several cells, all occupied. London wasn't a sleepy little town, and there was always someone in trouble with the law or one who just had to sleep off a bout of drunkenness. Dressed in a sheer lavender slip dress that layered just above the ankles with a black cape-coat and a feather-trimmed hat, Ginger caught their attention—each cell's occupant's head popping up like a weasel from a hole.

Basil jumped to his feet when he saw her.

"You have ten minutes," the sergeant said. He gave Basil a man-to-man look of understanding, then left them alone.

"Ginger," Basil said softly.

"Hello." Ginger had been Basil's close companion for many weeks, yet felt suddenly shy. "How are you?"

"I've been better, that's for sure."

"Indeed." Ginger let out a soft sigh, feeling heavy with the weight of their troubling situation.

Whispering, Basil spoke through the bars. "You must know I didn't kill Emelia."

Ginger whispered back. "I didn't believe it for a second."

Basil rubbed the back of his neck. "Who would do this? Who would want to kill her?"

Ginger got as close to the bars as she could without touching them. "We need to get inside the club."

Basil stopped short. "In what capacity?"

Ginger hesitated. She disliked the idea that came to her, and executing it would be rife with risk, but she couldn't think of any other way. "There's a vacancy now that—"

"No! Absolutely not."

"Basil, think about it. How else can we get inside information?"

"There must be some other way. Not only is what you're proposing dangerous, there's your reputation to consider."

Ginger had thought of that as well. If news broke that Lady Gold was discovered frequenting a dance club, it would ruffle London high society. Should it get out that she *danced*, well, it would be scandalous. Ambrosia would surely die of a heart attack. At the very least her grandmother-in-law's Victorian-era sensibilities would prevent the matron from ever leaving Hartigan House again.

"I'll go in disguise."

"No. Ginger, I don't want you getting involved like that."

"It's the only way we'll get the answers we seek," Ginger insisted. "You don't really think Morris is going to get to the bottom of this, do you?"

Basil sighed. Approaching the bars, he said, "I couldn't live with myself if something happened to you." His voice cracked. "I couldn't."

"I'll be careful, Basil."

"But Conway Sayer has seen you."

"He barely registered my existence." Ginger

wouldn't say it aloud, but she didn't think he was interested in women that way. "Besides, I'll wear a wig. It's amazing how a simple change in hair color throws people off the scent."

"No. I don't like it."

"I don't like it either, but—"

Basil snorted. "You're going to do it anyway."

"Yes. I'll do it to help you."

"I don't want this kind of help."

There was one benefit to having Basil locked behind bars. He couldn't stop her.

Ginger took a step back, offering a small, sad smile. "I'll be back. I promise." She raced away, but not before she heard Basil pound on the bars and swear under his breath.

THE NEXT MORNING, Ginger called a clandestine meeting with Felicia and Haley in her bedroom. They each sat in one of the two gold and white striped highback chairs, gaping at Ginger who, with Boss tucked under one arm, stood before them and relayed her plan.

"You've visited the club, Felicia. What can you tell me about it?"

"It's frequented by high-society men, mostly married, and young, single women, the kind the Americans call flappers."

Flappers were young women who defied the propriety of Victorian society in every conceivable way. Not only had the hair and hem length got shorter, the girls drank, smoked, danced, and caroused unsupervised.

Ginger would fit the definition to a degree, but Felicia even more so.

Felicia continued to tell her about the layout of the club. "There's a bar at the back of the room, a stage at the front where the girls perform, and the space between is filled with round tables and chairs."

"Did you ever see Emelia perform?" Haley asked.

Felicia hesitated. "I might have and not known it. The girls usually go to great lengths to change their appearance."

"Because they live a double life?" Ginger asked.

"It's quite likely," Felicia admitted.

Ginger put Boss on the floor, and he immediately jumped on the bed and curled into a ball. "What do you know of Mr. Sayer, the club manager?"

"I don't mind him," Felicia said. "He's there to do a job. Never paid me any notice the few times I was there."

"I need a costume," Ginger said.

"Are you really going to show your legs to a room full of strange men?" Felicia asked incredulously. "You were worried about my reputation. What of yours?"

"No one will know it's me."

Felicia was undaunted. "You'll know!"

"I'll do whatever it takes to clear Basil's name."

Felicia's look softened. "You're in love with him, aren't you?"

Ginger sniffed but didn't answer. Quite honestly, she wasn't sure anymore. But she did care for Basil and wouldn't stand around to watch him hang.

Haley intercepted. "What exactly do you hope to accomplish?"

Ginger set her gaze on her friend. "I'm going to snoop around a bit."

Haley frowned. "This sounds dangerous to me."

"Not any more dangerous than what the other dancers face," Ginger said. "Now, any ideas how to get a burlesque costume? I can't exactly ask Emma to sew one for me."

"Why not?" Felicia asked.

"I don't want anyone to know what I'm doing, especially my own employees. They'd never look at me the same way."

"I know!" Felicia said. "There's this terrific shop on Shaftesbury Avenue. I bet I can find something risqué there, and they'll make alterations for you as well. We're the same size," she added to Ginger's questioning look. "It would work."

The plan was set: Felicia would procure the costume and attend the club as herself and pretend not to know Ginger.

Ginger, in disguise, would ask Conway Sayer for a job. She knew there was a vacancy since news of the death of the dancer, her identity as the chief inspector's estranged wife, and Basil's subsequent arrest had hit the morning papers. Ambrosia had been quick to point it all out.

"And I thought he was such a nice man. Goes to show you never can tell what kind of evil lurks underneath."

"Grandmother!" Ginger snapped. "A man is innocent until proven guilty. Basil Reed did *not* kill his wife. It's a travesty that his reputation is being sullied in this manner."

Ambrosia, for once, had looked properly chastised.

Ginger dressed in a casual day dress with unassuming two-inch Oxfords. She thought it best to ask for work looking somewhat respectable—she had to face the public to get there, after all, but conveyed her dedication with heavy makeup, such as the doxies wore, at least according to Felicia.

It'd been several years since the last time Ginger had pretended to be someone she was not. Her days as Mademoiselle Antoinette LaFleur during the war in France were still fresh in her mind. It occurred to her she could resurrect that persona, minus her red hair.

With a French accent, she addressed her reflection in the full-length mirror. "Hello, *mon amie*."

Haley stepped into Ginger's bedroom in time to hear. She stilled as if she had spotted a ghost. "It's been a long time," Haley finally said.

The first time Haley and Ginger had met was in France. Ginger worked for the British secret service and Haley as a nurse. Haley had known Ginger as Mademoiselle LaFleur. The truth of Ginger's identity had been a shock to Haley when she had been solicited by Ginger to nurse Mr. Hartigan in the latter stages of his illness.

Before Ginger could respond, Felicia tapped on the door and burst inside. "The shop I was telling you about had a fantastic wig collection."

She placed a box on the bed, removed the lid, and lifted out a blonde wig with a long French braid. "What do you think?"

Ginger brightened. "It's perfect!"

After pinning her short locks off her face and placing the hair net over them, Ginger donned the wig. She smiled in the mirror, then faced Felicia and Haley.

"*Je suis* Antoinette LaFleur." Her French was impeccable. "I am a dancer."

Felicia clapped her hands. "Very believable. Lady Gold has completely disappeared!"

"*Bon*!" Ginger said. Eying the rest of the shopping bags she asked, "Is there more?"

"Yes. Your costume is ready." Felicia opened the box, tossing tissue paper to the floor, and produced a frock like a magician pulling a rabbit out of a hat. "*Voilà*."

It was shorter than anything Ginger had imagined, much shorter than what she had worn when she danced in France, but similar to what Emelia had been wearing.

She put the wig back in the box and covered her pinned hair with a tight-fitting cloche hat. Then she handed Felicia the keys to her Crossley. "Can you bring the Crossley to the front of the house?"

"Really? You trust me with your new motorcar?"

"Yes. You can take the costume out with you. I'm going to try to sneak out unseen."

"Brilliant!" Felicia disappeared like a flash of light before Ginger could change her mind. Had Ginger just made a mistake in judgment? She hoped not. Surely, not much damage could happen between the back lane and the front of the house.

Haley pushed loose curls behind her ears. "I have to get back to the hospital." Her gaze of concern locked on Ginger. "Please be careful."

"I will, I promise."

"I won't be able to sleep tonight until you return safely." Haley embraced Ginger before leaving with quick strides. She intended on catching the next wooden, red-painted double-decker bus.

Boss had watched Ginger's transformation in and out of her French alter ego with interest. Ginger scratched him behind the ears.

"I'm sorry I'm going to have to leave you behind, Bossy." Was it only yesterday she had taken Boss out on that fateful stroll? No wonder she felt heavy with fatigue. "Lizzie and Scout will take care of you."

Just as Ginger slipped down the stairs unnoticed, Matilda Hanson appeared on the landing.

"Lady Gold?"

Ginger paused, then turned halfway to show only her profile. "Is everything all right, Miss Hanson?"

"Yes. I just wanted to thank you for the library."

"You're welcome to read any book you like. I'm

afraid I'm in a hurry, but let's have tea together tomorrow."

Ginger slipped out of the door before Miss Hanson could engage her further. Poor girl. Hartigan House was a golden cage for her. Even with a houseful of women, she must be bored and lonely, since the rest of them were free to come and go and often did. She'd have to remind Haley to bring home another medical textbook for Miss Hanson to peruse.

Felicia drove up to the front gate with the Crossley, and Ginger got in. Ginger watched with some apprehension as her sister-in-law motored through the busy London streets but relaxed once she realised Felicia had everything under control. Ginger had to admit that Felicia might be a better driver than she was. However, Felicia had learned to drive on the left-hand side. How would she do driving in America?

"Thank you," Felicia said out of the blue.

"For what?"

"For taking me into your confidence."

"Of course."

"No, not of course. You and Haley have this special friendship, and I confess to having felt left out." She let out a breath. "I despise how childish that sounds."

Ginger swiveled to stare at Felicia. "My dear girl. I didn't know. I never meant to make you feel that way."

"I know. You are good-hearted, Ginger. Much more so than I."

"It's kind of you to say, Felicia, but I dare say it's not

true. You do know that you mean the world to me, don't you?"

Felicia simply shrugged.

"Well, you do. Every time I look at you, I see Daniel. No one else on earth can give that to me. Besides," Ginger placed a palm on Felicia's forearm, "you're my sister."

"*In-law.*"

"Pfft. *In-love*, you mean."

Felicia smiled, a twinkle in her eye, and Ginger knew in that instant Felicia finally believed it.

They approached the North Star, and Felicia parked the Crossley half a mile away. "You know what to do?"

"Go to the back entrance and ask for Mr. Sayer."

"Good. I'll see you there later tonight, *Mademoiselle LaFleur.*"

CHAPTER FOURTEEN

There were times during the war where Ginger had had to give convincing performances as various personas such as a farm girl, a young boy, a diplomat's wife and even a *prostituée*. So, no, this wouldn't be the first time Ginger had bared her legs in a room full of strange men.

But that had been years ago, and she was out of practice. She adjusted her wig, unused to the long braid hanging down her back, and shifted her holdall from one hand to the other. Then, she inhaled deeply to calm herself and knocked on the back entrance.

A response was slow in coming, and there was a minute or two when Ginger thought she'd been rash to get Felicia to drop her off and leave. She could catch a bus back though, and at least she was in disguise. Ginger knocked again, harder this time, and the door cracked open.

"What do you want?" Conway Sayer regarded her with thinly veiled contempt.

"Good morning, sir," Ginger began with a thick French accent. "I would like to apply for a job as a dancer. I understand that you have a possible new vacancy."

Mr. Sayer eyed her with suspicion. "What do you know about that?"

"Only what I've read in the morning paper."

"What's your name?"

"Antoinette."

"Do you have any experience, Miss Antoinette?"

"Oh, yes," Ginger answered truthfully. "I performed in France before coming to London."

Mr. Sayer eyed her up and down, not with personal interest, but with the eye of a businessman. He opened the door wider.

"Show me something?"

"I beg your pardon?"

"Sing or dance. Show me what you can do."

"Well, all right." Ginger smoothed out her skirt and cleared her throat before breaking out into "You've Got to See Mama Every Night." She'd been blessed with a good ear and a strong, clear voice. She jutted her hips to the right and threw her arms into the air as she held the final note.

"You've got the job, Miss Antoinette," Mr. Sayer said without a smile. Clearly, this was just a job to him.

The room was without windows, so the lighting

came solely from dim electric light bulbs. The club itself was classy enough with turquoise walls, polished walnut wood trim, and brass fixtures. Round tables dotted the carpeted floor with leather upholstered chairs pushed in neatly.

A young man was setting up the bar, the muscles of his biceps strained against his white shirt as he dried glasses and put them on the shelves behind him. Ginger thought he might work double-duty to prevent fights and rabble-rousing. He watched her with clear blue eyes as Mr. Sayer showed her the room.

"New lass, boss?" he called out.

Mr. Sayer scowled. "Not that's anything to you."

Ginger approached the barman and extended her hand. "I'm Antoinette."

The barman's eyes squinted. "French?"

"Oui, monsieur."

"Delightful." He approached, and Ginger noted a distinctive limp. War wound, likely. He extended a hand. "Billy Foster."

Ginger smiled flirtatiously. If she hoped to gain any information from this man, she had to play the game his way. "It's a pleasure to meet you, Monsieur Foster."

"Miss Antoinette!" Conway Sayer growled.

Ginger giggled and skipped after the club manager. "*Je suis désolée!*"

Mr. Sayer led her to a connecting hallway. "This takes you to the dressing room."

Ginger had been here earlier with Mr. Sayer as

LEE STRAUSS

herself, and she was pleased that the disgruntled man had shown no signs of recognition. He opened the cupboard that had belonged to Emelia, now empty.

"You can put your things here."

"Does it lock?"

"No need. Our girls are honest." He pierced her with a look that challenged her to be anything but honest herself.

"Of course, Mr. Sayer."

They were interrupted by a youthful and pretty redhead who entered the dressing room carrying a small suitcase and a large square shape that looked like a type of bird cage, but it was impossible to say as a thin blanket was draped over the top.

"Cindy," Mr. Sayer said, his relief almost palpable. "This is Antoinette. Show her the ropes." He disappeared before Cindy could object.

Cindy's brown eyes assessed Ginger competitively.

"Hello," Ginger said. She found it strangely disconcerting facing the dancer. It was almost like looking in the mirror. She was the same height, of similar build, and wore her red hair in the same style bob as Ginger.

"You're French," Cindy said. A statement, not a question.

"Oui."

Cindy went to one of the mirrors. The countertop was filled with perfumes and other items that Ginger assumed were personal to Cindy.

Cindy flicked a wrist toward an empty chair. "You can sit there."

"It doesn't belong to anyone?" Ginger suspected it had been Emelia's spot.

"Not anymore."

"Oh, sounds like a story there."

"She met her maker last night." Cindy shrugged as if Emelia meant no more to her than a traveling salesman.

"How awful," Ginger said. She pulled out the chair and sat. "Do you know what happened?"

Cindy shook her head. "Likely a disgruntled lover." She leaned in closer to the mirror and applied a dark-red lipstick. She smacked her lips then added, "It's an occupational hazard."

Indeed. Ginger wondered what had led such a pretty girl to this kind of life. For that matter, she wondered what had drawn Emelia Reed.

"Do you have a bird in there?" Ginger inquired, motioning to the cage.

Cindy paused, mid-brush stroke. One corner of her full lips pulled up into a wry smile. "My pet. It's sleeping right now," she added as if to warn Ginger off from taking a peek.

Two more girls arrived, one blonde and the other brunette, and each solemnly claimed a mirror. "Those Irish lasses are joined at the hip," Cindy said softly. "Say they're just flatmates, but I have my suspicions." She then raised her voice to make introductions.

"Sorcha and Nuala, this is Destiny's replacement, Antoinette."

"*Bonsoir*," Ginger said.

"Frenchie, eh?" Nuala said with a clear Irish roll of the 'r'. "Mind you're p's and q's, and we'll get along just fine."

"Sorcha and Nuala do a cops and robbers bit," Cindy explained. "Gets the fellas laughing. What do you do?"

"French maid," Ginger said, sweetly. She pulled a feather duster from Haley's holdall.

Ginger's new colleagues didn't look impressed.

"I heard about the misfortune of the dancer, Destiny, was it?" Ginger said. "How sad. Did you girls know her well?"

Nuala harrumphed. "Destiny kept herself to herself. Too posh for the likes of us."

"She wasn't one of us," Sorcha added. She sat in front of her mirror which was topped by a row of electric light bulbs and opened a jar of face cream. Ginger caught the label, *Jeune et Belle*. The scent of the cream reminded her of something.

Yes. Emelia's cheap French perfume. Had she been using this face cream? Did she get it from Sorcha?

"What kind of routine did Destiny do?" Ginger asked

Sorcha rubbed the face cream vigorously onto her cheeks, forehead, and around her mouth. "Some dull shepherdess routine."

"Did you get on with her?"

Cindy narrowed her dark gaze. "Why are you so interested in her?"

Ginger looked Cindy boldly in the eyes. "I confess I'm a little obsessed with the morbid." She turned to

92

the newcomers. "Do you know how the poor thing died?"

The girls shook their heads.

"I bet that toff did her in," Nuala said.

"What toff?" Ginger asked.

"Jonathon Phillips," Sorcha answered. "Ain't he an American?"

"A diplomat," Cindy said.

Nuala smirked. "Quite handsome for an older man. I adore his accent."

"Not as handsome as Billy," Sorcha said with a swoon.

"The barman?" Ginger asked.

"Sorcha is soft on him," Cindy explained.

"Cindy!" Sorcha protested.

Cindy turned her back to Sorcha and lowered her voice. "Now that Destiny's gone, she might actually have a chance."

"Billy and Destiny?" Ginger said, leaning forward. "He must be devastated by her death."

Cindy shrugged. "He's a man. There're plenty of fish in the sea."

PEEKING out into the audience from stage left, Ginger spotted Felicia and Haley in attendance. Felicia wore a cherry-red evening gown—a sheer embroidered crepe de chine over a silk slip of the same color. An elegant bow sat on the dropped waist. A flamboyant scarlet feather burst from her headband.

Haley was a pure surprise. Ginger hadn't thought she would be coming along. And she had dressed in something other than her trademark tweed suit: a feminine but straightforward frock trimmed in sequins. Ginger had never seen Haley wear so much makeup before. She hardly recognized her. The two were seated at a table near the front. With them was a well-dressed, eye-catching man with a pencil mustache. Maybe mid-thirties? Felicia had a cocktail in one hand and with the other, she rubbed the rim with a long fingernail painted the same red as her feather. She leaned in close to the gentleman and fluttered heavily made-up eyelashes. Even from her distance behind the curtain, Ginger could see the hooded glassy look of lust reflect in the gent's eyes. Ginger found the exchange alarming. Without glancing Felicia's way, Haley pinched her from under the table, a move that had Felicia jumping away from the womanizing gentleman, and Ginger grinned in approval.

Cindy sneaked up from behind. "Another full house."

Ginger grabbed at her heart, recovering from having been startled. Cindy continued. "Probably news of Destiny's death has got out. Looks like you're not the only morbid one in London."

"*Histoire et règles de la tragédie.*" At Cindy's confused look, Ginger translated. "History and rules of tragedy."

Cindy frowned then said. "You're on after Nuala and Sorcha. I close the night."

The dance routines were just a warm up to the fraternizing that happened afterwards. It was Billy's job to sell as much alcohol as possible. The dancers, well, it was up to them how they made extra money that night.

CHAPTER FIFTEEN

*G*inger watched Nuala and Sorcha's routine from her spot in the wings. They made a show of Nuala's copper. Dressed in an overly long police jacket with a helmet over her dark cropped hair, Nuala chased Sorcha's robber. Sorcha's costume consisted of a man's brown waistcoat with her honey-blonde hair tucked into a flat, newsboy cap. The stage wasn't overly wide, and the girls added creative dance moves to spin across it. Nuala had a rubber truncheon which elicited laughter each time she whacked Sorcha over the head. With each round, they'd pause centre stage and feign heat, and one piece of clothing would come off starting with the helmet and hat until the two were in only a corset and bloomers. It ended with Nuala handcuffing a stumbling Sorcha and dragging her off stage.

The audience cheered and applauded. Ginger's

stomach flittered with nerves. She'd been running the routine—one she'd performed in France during wartime—through her head all day. She hoped she remembered it.

She glanced at the piano player, a Jamaican man with silky brown skin and deep dark eyes that twinkled with his love of music, and he started the tune she'd asked him to play. The electric lights over the stage blinded her to the audience, but she could make out the tables at the front. She almost burst out laughing at the expression on Haley and Felicia's faces.

Dressed skimpily in her French maid costume, Ginger began by sweeping the floor with a broom, when the music changed to a waltz, the broom became her dance partner. She pretended to get it caught in her apron string, and the apron came off. Ginger feigned surprise, then picked up her next prop, a large, grey feather duster. She mimed dusting different items when the tempo sped up to jazz, and Ginger broke into the Charleston—a new addition to her routine since the war. She kicked her feet up, dropping the duster as she raised her hands. The blonde braid of her wig swung along her back, and Ginger used this distraction to pull on her dress. It had a breakaway back, and it fell to the floor leaving Ginger in her frilly bloomers and full-body corset. She covered her body as if she were embarrassed, swooped down to collect her dress and scurried off the stage, pausing briefly. She winked at the crowd while raising her back foot before disappearing out of sight.

Ginger stopped to catch her breath, registering the hoots and howls of the audience that followed her. She grinned to herself as she slipped her costume back on. She still had it.

Cindy, dressed as an Indian princess with a long black wig and a colorful, sheer, floor-length sari, waited nearby with the covered cage. Unlike Nuala and Sorcha, who had waited to go on with whisky-induced smiles and giggles, Cindy's expression was serious. She breathed in deeply and shook out her arms as if to calm herself.

"Is everything all right?" Ginger asked.

Cindy glanced at her sharply. "Please don't speak to me."

Everyone dealt with nerves differently. Ginger said no more.

The song selection had a hint of the east, the high notes fingered lightly like the tone of a penny flute. Cindy had placed the covered cage onto a small table set to one side and began dancing gracefully, palms pressed together prayer-fashion in front of her chest, hips floating. It was fascinating to watch her, and Ginger could see immediately why Cindy closed the show. Soon, the sari fell to the floor to the hoots and cheers of the crowd. In just her corset and knickers, she floated next to the cage, which had been forgotten until now. Cindy snapped the blanket off with flair. Ginger gasped. Cindy's bird wasn't a bird at all. It was a snake. Tri-colored—red, black and pale yellow. Was *this* the murder weapon?

Chairs near the front of the stage shuffled back when Cindy made a show of opening the cage. She slowly reached inside and gathered the snake's long body into her hands. She eased it around her neck, holding the head in one hand and the tail in the other. Her hips continued to sway to the music. After a few minutes with the crowd collectively holding their breath, Cindy placed the snake back into its cage. Cindy finished her routine by bowing, giving everyone a good look at her ample cleavage. The she picked up the cage and exited stage left.

Ginger joined in the applause. "Very impressive," she said as the snake dancer approached.

Cindy's face broke into a smile. "Thank you. It's always a thrill for me. I feel as high as if I had smoked an opium pipe!"

"Oh. Does that go on around here?" Ginger said, looking interested.

Cindy shrugged. "Sometimes."

"Is your snake dangerous?"

"Jake? Only if you don't know how to handle him." She patted Ginger's arm and smiled wryly. "He's a wild scarlet. Harmless. I'm not crazy enough to dance with a poisonous snake."

"Where did you get such an exotic creature? It's surely not native to England."

Cindy shot Ginger a sideways glance. "You'd be amazed at what you can buy at Harrods Animal Kingdom."

The dancers mingled in with the crowd. Cindy,

Nuala, and Sorcha seemed to have regulars they headed for, plopping themselves carelessly on the men's laps.

Ginger headed casually to Felicia and Haley's table, having locked eyes with the gentleman there. His were a lusty, icy-blue and Ginger immediately distrusted him.

"You're new," he said with a lazy smile. His accent was notably American, but not from New England. She felt providence had guided her to the diplomat.

He pulled away from the table to offer his lap.

Ginger deftly ignored the man's suggestive move and pulled up an empty chair. Cindy pushed past, bumping into Ginger's chair and didn't bother to say excuse me. Cindy's eyes latched on the man. At first, Ginger thought she would take the proffered lap, but instead, she whispered hotly in the man's ear, and by the angry glint in her eye, Ginger doubted her message contained sweet nothings.

The diplomat grunted, giving Cindy a nasty look, before readjusting his smarmy grin for Ginger's sake.

Ginger reached out her bare hand. "I'm Antoinette."

"*Bonsoir, jolie dame*. I'm John Phillips. I enjoyed your dance very much."

Ginger stared up from under her eyelashes. "*Merci*."

"Nothing compared to the snake dancer," Felicia said with disdain.

Haley pitched in, feigning additional displeasure, "I'm not a fan of reptiles. I mean what would happen if the thing got away?"

"What happened to that other dancer, I wonder," Felicia said. She tapped the man on the arm. "Mr. Phillips, you must know who I mean?"

Ginger was impressed by Felicia's initiative, giving her the man's name and bringing Emelia's case into the conversation.

Mr. Phillips nodded. "The Shepherdess." He leaned toward Ginger. "A similar routine to yours, Miss Antoinette, though I confess, I enjoyed yours better."

"So kind of you to say, Monsieur Phillips. Were you not a fan of Mademoiselle Destiny?"

"Oh, certainly." His lips tugged up. "She definitely had her qualities."

"Do you know what happened to her?"

Jonathon Phillips' smile fell. "I heard she died."

"Oh, no!" Ginger exclaimed, keeping to character. "So sad."

"Apparently, she'd been *murdered*," Felicia said as though caught up in the scandalous story.

"It's not safe to walk alone after dark," Haley added with a note of self-righteousness. "Especially in London."

Felicia scoffed. "It's no more dangerous than New York!"

Haley sniffed in return. "Both cities are unfriendly once the sun sets."

"I only know what the papers, say," Mr. Phillips said. "A dog walker discovered her body in Kensington Gardens." He took a long pull of his whisky. "Now let's talk about more pleasurable things, shall we?"

CHAPTER SIXTEEN

*G*inger was finishing her breakfast and sneaking bits of bacon to Boss, who watched her with bright eyes and the stub of his tail wagging in anticipation when Pippins entered the morning room.

"Telephone call for you, madam. It's Miss Higgins."

Haley had gone to work early. She must have been exhausted after staying late at the club the night before. Ginger felt a twinge of guilt as she shifted from the table and hurried to her study.

"Hello, Haley." Ginger could picture her in her position in the mortuary. "I'm assuming you have news?"

"Excessive proteins were found in the blood sample."

"What does that mean?" Ginger twisted the cord of the telephone through her fingers, nervous with anticipation.

"Excessive proteins indicate the presence of snake venom," Haley answered.

"Interesting," Ginger said. "Cindy told me her snake was harmless."

"Could she be lying?"

"Anything is possible. Have you called Scotland Yard with the news?"

"I just got off the telephone with them. Morris wasn't available, so I left a message."

"What about Emelia's clothes?"

"Nothing noteworthy," Haley said. "Everything was in good condition, no spills, tears or stains."

"Good to know. I'm heading to the Yard now," Ginger said, feeling excited. "I have to tell Superintendent Morris what I know about Cindy's snake."

"And break the good inspector out of jail," Haley added. Ginger could sense the mirth in her voice.

"Yes, indeed! Everyone's favorite burlesque dancer just jumped to the top of the suspect list."

As GINGER SPED through the streets of London, her mind filled with thoughts of the previous night and the things she'd done and learned. She was only vaguely aware of the aggravated horns honking in her wake. Cindy, whatever her real name was, didn't like to be upstaged. Imagined or not, Emelia had become the snake dancer's enemy. If anyone knew how to retrieve snake venom from her snake without getting bitten— assuming it was indeed poisonous—it would be her.

Ginger shouldn't have been surprised at Superintendent Morris' lack of appreciation for her revelation. She felt like a schoolgirl in the headmistress' office, standing with hands clasped in front of her as the superintendent leaned over his desk, red in the face.

"I told you to stay out of police business!"

"Yes, but—"

"I've got a man assigned to that club."

"So, he must've seen Cindy and Jake."

The V in between Morris' bushy brows deepened. "Who are Cindy and Jake?"

"The snake dancer and her snake."

Morris growled. "You're saying you suspect this Cindy's snake bit Emelia Reed?" Obviously, he hadn't got Haley's message.

"All I know is that Emelia Reed was bitten by a snake, and a dancer at the same club that Mrs. Reed danced at has a snake. It's worth investigating."

"Yes, yes, yes. No need to tell me how to do my job, Lady Gold." He let out a frustrated breath. "I expect this clears Reed. For the moment anyway." The superintendent almost looked disappointed. "I'll call the station."

Ginger smiled. "Let them know I'll pick him up." Her stomach twisted with nerves at seeing Basil again. She was still wary of Basil's emotional state and protective of her own. Yet, she was happy he was about to be released.

Basil looked a little worse for wear with dark shadows under his eyes, a wrinkled shirt, and salt and pepper bristles forming on his chin. He inhaled when he saw Ginger.

"You're a sight for sore eyes."

"I'm just happy to see you on this side of the bars."

"As am I," Basil said, relieved.

"I'll drive you home."

"That would be appreciated. I'm in desperate need of a bath and a shave."

Ginger agreed.

The station constable called after them. "Excuse me, Chief Inspector. Superintendent Morris wanted me to give you a message." The constable cleared his throat looking distinctly uncomfortable, and Ginger figured the message was unpleasant to the messenger. She was right.

"He said, you might be off the hook, for now, Mr. Reed, but don't leave town. And keep off this case if you want a job to come back to."

"Understood, Constable," Basil said. "Thank you."

"Oh, and he said, to keep your lady friend in line." He glanced at Ginger sheepishly. "Forgive me, madam. His words not mine."

Ginger clenched her teeth. She could keep *herself* in line, Superintendent Morris, thank you very much.

THE RIDE to Mayfair was quiet.

Basil broke the silence. "You were at the North Star last night?"

He knew that had been Ginger's plan. She replied simply. "Yes."

"You *danced*?"

"I took Destiny's place in the program."

Basil ducked his chin and shook his head. "I wish you hadn't."

"I know. But it was the fastest way for me to get to know the dancers. It was how I found Jake the snake, which led to your release I might add."

Basil sighed. "I thank you for that."

Ginger pulled up in front of Basil's house. She faced him with a tilt of her head. "Are you *really* going to stay off the case?"

He snorted. "Not on your life."

Ginger grinned and followed Basil inside.

CHAPTER SEVENTEEN

One thing Ginger had to appreciate her stepmother, Sally Hartigan, for was that she had insisted that Ginger and her half-sister Louisa learned to cook. At least the basics. Sally didn't teach them herself, of course. They had a full-time cook to take on that thankless task.

While Basil bathed, Ginger took liberties in his kitchen. She imagined he must be starving by now, not-withstanding lousy prison food. She found eggs, a tin of kippers, tomatoes, and a dish of butter in the pantry. A loaf of bread sat on the counter, growing stale but suitable for frying. Before long, the place was filled with the aroma of melted butter. The egg whites touched the fish, and after a few minutes, she flipped them to the satisfying sound of sizzling. Meanwhile, she sliced the bread and tomatoes, then fried the bread in the same pan in the egg and kipper juices.

When Basil entered the kitchen, he looked remarkably better with fresh clothes and smooth, newly shaven skin. The table was set and breakfast waiting.

"You did this?" Basil asked. Ginger didn't know if she should feel slighted by this incredulousness, but then, a lady of her status rarely knew her way around a kitchen.

"I'm a woman of many talents."

Basil chuckled. "That you are, Lady Gold."

He approached her then, past the gas stove and around the round wooden kitchen table. The frying pan wasn't the only thing to heat up. The air in the room crackled and snapped. Basil touched her shoulder, and Ginger couldn't stop the involuntary shiver. She should've been looking up into his eyes, reading what was there. Longing? Sadness? Confusion? But all she could manage was to stare at her Italian designer shoes. *Was that a scuff on the toe?*

He closed the space between them. "Are you all right with this?"

Ginger tensed. She wanted it to be. She desperately wanted to go back in time to three days before, when she had thought Basil truly loved her. But now she couldn't get the image of Basil weeping over Emelia out of her head. "I'm . . . not sure."

Basil slumped, and he stepped back. "I understand. Now let's eat before this delectable meal gets cold."

Conversation quickly turned to the case. With their focus on that, and not on *themselves*, Ginger's stomach finally agreed to open up to receive the work of her hands.

"What else did you learn from your evening exploits?" There was an edge to Basil's voice Ginger ignored.

"Well, you've met the club manager, Conway Sayer."

"So, not a likely suspect," Basil said as he cut into his kipper. "Not a romantic one, anyway."

"The barman is a bit of a hefty man. He's built more like a guard than a server. He has a leg injury of some sort—I'm assuming from the war. He made me uncomfortable." Ginger pressed a napkin against her lips. Butter was marvelous, but left its mark.

"More tea?" Basil asked, lifting the teapot.

"Please." Ginger added a little sugar and stirred. She filled Basil in on Nuala and Sorcha. "Quite honestly, they seemed a little dim-witted to pull something like this off. Though looks are often deceiving, and they did have access to Cindy's snake."

Ginger hesitated, and Basil noticed.

"Is there more?"

"There is a man, a frequent guest at the club. Apparently, *Destiny* was a favorite of his."

"Did you speak to this man?"

"Yes. Felicia and Haley were with me at his table."

Basil relaxed a little after that information was offered. "And?"

"Nothing of note. I was told by Cindy that he was a diplomat."

"What country?"

"America."

"What type of snake did you say it was?"

"Cindy says it's a wild scarlet."

Basil's dark brow shot up. "A breed found in America, I dare say."

"Also sold at Harrods, apparently."

They were interrupted by the telephone ringing from another room. Basil excused himself. Ginger stepped to the passageway and strained to hear Basil's side of the conversation, but he wasn't adding much to it. It ended quickly. "Thank you, Constable."

Ginger remained standing and waited. Basil returned shortly.

"Any news?" Ginger asked. The call was from a constable, and Ginger could only assume it was the police.

"I have a fellow keeping me posted."

"Apart from the superintendent's knowledge?"

Basil nodded and returned to the table. Ginger followed.

"Cynthia Webb, also known as Cindy, is the new prime suspect. They've got men trailing her. No suspicious activity so far."

"Cindy has means and opportunity, but does she have a motive?" Ginger asked. "Besides a reasonable amount of competition."

"No, not that we've ascertained. And if we wait for Morris to investigate, they may never find one."

CHAPTER EIGHTEEN

*G*inger clung to her hat as she and Basil ran across the busy road, narrowly dodging a speeding lorry.

"Where does one go to enquire about exotic pets?" she asked when they were safely on the other side.

"I can only think of one place." Basil looked at her. "Would you allow me to drive?"

Ginger grinned. Basil's former confident self was peeking through. "If you like," she said, handing him the keys. "But I warn you, you'll be ruined for your Austin."

Basil grinned back. "I'll take my chances."

He steered them toward Hyde Park, and Ginger wondered for a moment if Basil was taking her home, but then he turned down Brompton Road in Knightsbridge.

"Of course!" Ginger said. "Harrods Animal Kingdom. I've heard of it, of course, but never made it past the ladies' clothing sections."

They passed a white-topped black Harrods lorry, and Ginger wondered if it might be holding an exotic animal that had made Harrods Animal Kingdom world famous. A baby elephant or cheetah, perhaps?

Harrods was a London jewel, a luxurious monument to mankind's desire to shop and live well. The building was breathtaking in its size alone, six stories of grandeur covering several acres. It would take a week to visit every department.

The pavements were busy with shoppers coming and going, and getting a spot to park took ingenuity, having to outmaneuver red double-decker wooden buses, horses and carts, and pedestrians.

Inside was like entering a mystical world, one of fantasy and mythology. Crystal and gold, lights and shiny reflective surfaces. Colorful and artful displays of expensive and fashionable jewelry, clothing, and every kind of trinket imaginable.

They took the lift up to the fourth floor, and Ginger couldn't conceal her amazement at what she saw when the lift operator retracted the expandable metal door.

"Oh, mercy!"

When the press said Harrods Animal Kingdom rivaled London Zoo, they weren't far wrong, if the zoo only held exotic baby animals captive.

A baby elephant lifted his trunk and trumpeted into the air as Ginger approached.

Ginger felt like bursting with the pleasure of seeing

such a magnificent animal up close. "What a beautiful creature!"

"Indeed," Basil said. "A shame it's not with its family in its natural habitat.

Ginger had to agree with that sentiment but couldn't deny the thrill of being this close.

There were other exotic animals. Lion cubs and cheetah kittens, as adorable as their domesticated cousins yet so much more dramatic.

A salesman secured a collar to one of the lean cheetah kittens and handed the leash to its new owner. "He's so adorable!" The woman declared loudly. She wore a coat with a spotted fur collar and Ginger couldn't help but wonder what her new pet thought about that.

Ginger gaped at the other animals on display for sale to whoever had the means and courage to make a purchase: camels, anteaters, crocodiles.

"What happens when these pets get too large and strong to handle?" Ginger asked.

"Most end up in London Zoo," Basil said. "The more fortunate ones are returned to the wild."

They watched the lady walk out of Harrods with her cheetah on a leash. Ginger couldn't help but shake her head. The salesman, happy with having just made a sale, approached them with a big smile.

"Hello. I'm Mr. Long. Can I help you find something?"

"Do you sell snakes?"

"Of course. Are you looking for Indian, Australian, or African?"

"American. Have you sold any wild scarlet snakes recently?" Basil asked.

"Our sales and client information is strictly confidential."

Basil took out his identification card. "I'm Chief Inspector Reed. This is a murder inquiry."

"Murder?" The salesman's adam's apple bobbed. "Suffocation or bite?"

Basil grimaced. "Bite."

"I wish I could help, but we haven't sold any snakes for a few weeks. No wait, we did sell a wild scarlet." He frowned at them. "The scarlets aren't venomous, though."

"Did you sell it to a man or woman?" Basil asked.

"Lady, young, like you madam," he smiled at Ginger appreciatively.

"Does the name Cynthia Webb sound familiar?" Ginger asked.

"Yes, I believe that's her." Mr. Long's finger went to his chin as a new thought occurred to him. "The wild scarlet looks a lot like the coral snake. Same red, black and yellow markings, only in a different sequence. The Americans have a little riddle to help distinguish them. Red-touch-black, venom-lack; red-touch-yellow, kill a fellow."

"Is it possible that Miss Webb was sold the wrong snake?" Basil asked.

The man jerked back with a look of disbelief.

"Never! We are very careful and professional here at Harrods Animal Kingdom. Such a thing would never happen."

Though Harrods Animal Kingdom was famous for its exotic animals, it was also the place to go for the more domesticated types and animal supplies. Ginger was surprised to see Jonathan Phillips in the bovine section. Grabbing Basil by the sleeve, she pulled him behind a large pillar before Mr. Phillips spotted them.

Basil shot her a questioning look.

"It's John Phillips, the diplomat."

Basil's gaze grew dark and narrow with distaste. Ginger could only imagine he was picturing his wife with the American.

Mr. Phillips exchanged cash with the cashier.

"What's he buying?" Basil asked.

Ginger squinted at the square, green tin, feeling perplexed. "It looks like bag balm."

Basil stiffened. "A bomb?"

"Not bomb, *balm*. It's a salve for softening the udder of a cow."

Ginger was familiar with the product as it was often used in Boston, and she'd even seen it in use in France during the war.

"What on earth would an American diplomat living in London need udder salve for?" Basil said.

Ginger shrugged. "Good question. Maybe he has friends on a farm?"

Ginger and Basil casually followed the mysterious diplomat past the monkeys and kittens to the lift lobby.

With heads lowered and eyes averted, they crowded inside the gilded lift keeping to the opposite end from Mr. Phillips' position as it slowly lowered to the main floor. In other circumstances, Ginger would've stopped to admire the frocks and shoes on display in the ladies wear department, but today she didn't dare let her eyes stray from Mr. Phillips' back.

Outside, Jonathon Phillips flagged down a black taxicab. Ginger and Basil hurried to follow him, Basil continuing to commandeer Ginger's Crossley.

"He turned onto Knightsbridge," Ginger said, willing Basil to catch up.

"I see him," Basil said.

They followed the taxicab through Belgravia flanked on either side by three- and four-story façades of red brick and white stone, circling around Belgrave Square Park to Grosvenor Gardens.

"Isn't this where the American Embassy is located?" Ginger asked.

Basil nodded. He slowed to a stop behind two motorcars and a view-obscuring bus. "Can you see him?"

Ginger craned her neck and stuck her head out of the window as far as she could.

"He's getting out."

The traffic moved forward in time for them to watch Mr. Phillips enter the American Embassy.

"I guess he's telling the truth about that," Ginger said.

CHAPTER NINETEEN

*B*asil had tried to talk Ginger out of dancing that night at the North Star for her job as Antoinette. She was confident the killer was linked to the club somehow, so she couldn't risk getting sacked by not showing up. Getting inside and behind the scenes was too great an asset to ignore.

Haley and Felicia insisted on coming, which Ginger didn't mind. But so did Basil. This Ginger minded. However, if she was defying Morris and investigating on her own, she couldn't very well keep Basil from doing the same.

"What are you going to do, Antoinette?" Sorcha asked. "Conway doesn't like us to do the same thing twice in a row."

"Can I borrow from the costume rack?" Ginger asked.

Cindy nodded. "Feel free."

Ginger thumbed through the outfits and found something that would work for a Heidi-type character. There was even a dark curly wig, but Ginger had to make sure she was well hidden behind the dressing screen when she removed her blonde one. Once she had dressed in the altered Swiss outfit—much shorter than normal and landing shockingly at mid-thigh, she startled her colleagues by breaking out into a convincing yodel. The girls nodded with approval.

Ginger eyed the snake cage tucked behind Cindy. It was covered so she couldn't test out Mr. Long's riddle.

"I'm looking for a new flat," Ginger announced. "Where do you girls live?"

"We're in the Johnson building," Nuala said into the mirror. "Just around the corner."

"All of you?"

Sorcha answered. "The club owner owns it too. Talk to Conway."

Conway brought them a simple meal of hot steak and kidney pie. "I'm docking your pay," he said without feeling.

Sorcha muttered, "Eejit."

Ginger was starving. She dug into her meat pie and ran a new dance routine through her mind until she was certain of how her act would go. She could feel the energy from the main room fill the building as the numbers grew. Conway gave them a thirty-minute warning to get ready.

They fussed with hair and makeup in the mirrors, double-checked their costumes.

"Are you dancing with Jake again?" Ginger asked, hoping to get a quick glimpse of the reptile.

"You heard Sorcha. Conway doesn't like us to do the same act twice in a row."

A rising cacophony of voices from the main area of the club filtered into backstage. Ginger could sense the energy fill the place as more drinks were consumed and anticipation for the dancers increased.

Nuala and Sorcha prepared to go on first, but before the first note was played by the pianist, a commotion interrupted Conway Sayer's carefully planned out agenda. Superintendent Morris' bear-like growl overwhelmed the rest of the voices.

"I'm looking for Miss Cynthia Webb," he bellowed. His heavy footsteps echoed across the stage, and it would only be seconds before he got to the girls. Cindy's eyes were wide with fright, and she dashed for the back door. Ginger pretended to jump out of her way, but instead pushed a prop in front of the dancer, slowing her enough that Morris' men reached her before she could get away.

"Miss Webb," Morris said. "You need to come with us."

"Why? I didn't do nothing!"

Sorcha and Nuala froze to the spot, jaws unhinged as they watched Cindy being handcuffed. Ginger stepped back and kept her face turned. Having Morris recognize her right now would be disastrous.

"You're under arrest, Miss Webb," Morris said, "on suspicion of murdering Mrs. Emelia Reed."

"The snake sir?" his sergeant said.

"Yes. We need your snake, Miss Webb."

"It's in the dressing room," Ginger mumbled, keeping her French accent intact.

Cindy glared at her with a look of betrayal.

Morris and his men took Cindy and her snake out of the back entrance. Conway took centre stage to calm the crowd and told them the dancers just needed to regroup and would be out shortly, and to avail themselves of the bar.

Nuala and Sorcha were clearly shaken, or at least made a good show of appearing shaken. Conway had even brought them each a shot of whisky to calm their nerves.

"It's coming off your pay," he said.

"Do you think she did it?" Ginger prodded once Conway had left them alone. "Do you think Cindy *keeled* Destiny?"

Sorcha gulped back her shot of whisky. "Cindy didn't like Destiny and didn't hide the fact."

"Why?" Ginger tilted toward the duo with a look of curiosity and a love of gossip. "What did Destiny do to her?"

"Stole Mr. Phillips, is what she did," Sorcha said. "Before Destiny came along, he showered all his attention on Cindy."

Had Cynthia Webb killed Emelia out of jealousy?

Nuala slammed her shot glass down. "I don't know if Cindy killed Destiny or not, but at least this will take her down a peg or two. So full of herself, talking down to us all the time like she's the Queen's lady."

Destiny hadn't been the only one at odds with Cindy. Nuala seemed the type who'd set a fellow competitor up for a crime she didn't commit.

Conway returned, clapping his hands. "Chop, chop. Time to get on with the show."

When the curtain finally opened, Nuala stood centre stage hidden behind two huge fans made of fluffy pink feathers. Matching plumes sprouted from the white cap on her head and off the backside of her white costume. Pink-colored stockings completed her bird-look.

She kept her back from the crowd, hiding her "tail." She saved that feature for the "bird and hunter" portion of the routine. Nuala tantalized the audience who showed their appreciation with hoots and cheers.

Part way through Sorcha tiptoed in, crouched low, with a wooden prop shaped like a rifle. Nuala scampered about like a frightened fowl, losing tail feathers as she went and by the end, neither girl wore much.

Despite the bawdiness, Ginger smiled. The girls were talented.

The curtain closed, and the girls giggled as they ran off. Ginger took her position. The curtain opened as her name was announced. "Our French darling, Antoinette!"

Ginger swept her way to the middle of the stage, smiling to the crowd. Immediately, she found Haley and Felicia sitting front and centre, Mr. Phillips sitting like a peacock in between two hens. They weren't who she was looking for.

Then she saw him, sitting alone at a table at the back. His eyes looked black in the dim lighting of the club, troubled and disapproving. Even though Ginger knew he'd be there, that he was seeing her wearing nothing more than that of a cheap doxy, made her flush with embarrassment.

She stumbled briefly before her professionalism resurfaced. She wasn't Ginger Gold. She was Antoinette LaFleur. She wasn't doing this for the thrill, but to get to the bottom of Emelia's murder and to help Basil move on.

CHAPTER TWENTY

*W*hen the curtain fell, a few hecklers were calling for Cynthia Webb. "We want Cindy! We want Jake the snake!" Word of Cynthia's backstage arrest had failed to reach the main room.

"Go out there and calm the men down," Conway instructed. "Use whatever means necessary."

"But there're only three of us?" Sorcha complained.

"I'm working on rectifying that situation."

His comment shut Sorcha up. Tonight, she and Nuala were stars—next week they could be outshone by newcomers.

Ginger mused. Had *they* killed Emelia and framed Cindy in the process? For a chance to become small-time stars? Maybe this duo weren't as harmless as they appeared.

The three, with big smiles pasted on their faces, headed into the crowd. Mr. Phillip's gaze never left

Ginger, and he made a show of patting his lap. Ginger stroked his shoulder playfully but continued by. She could feel the diplomat's glare pierce her back. She made a show of teasing all the tables as she wiggled by until she reached Basil.

"Hello, handsome," she said loud enough for the neighboring tables to hear. "Are you new to North Star?"

Basil smirked

Ginger addressed the room, "A North Star first-timer, everyone!"

The room erupted in a roar of hilarity while Basil rolled his eyes.

As if on cue, the piano player attacked the ivory keys with a raucous rendition of "Toot Toot Tootsie Goodbye," loud enough for her and Basil to converse without being overheard.

"What went on backstage?" Basil said. "I was worried Morris had found out you were back there." His jaw twitched with frustration.

Ginger patted his hand. "He didn't recognize me. He arrested Cynthia. I don't know what he thinks he has on her that's not circumstantial."

"Do you think she's guilty?"

"I don't know. The constable took the snake before I could get a look at it. Perhaps your man at the Yard will be able to tell you if it's a wild scarlet or a coral snake."

"Yes." Basil watched Sorcha and Nuala work the room. "I want to talk to those dancers. Can you introduce me?"

"Yes, but we have to make it look casual and natural. You don't want them guessing you're a detective. Really, you need to relax. You've got the Yard written all over your face."

She reached over to massage his shoulders. "What did you think of my show?"

Basil pulled at his collar. "As a man—I loved it. As your . . . friend, I didn't like it one bit."

Friend. Would their relationship to each other ever be appropriately defined?

"Let's go to the bar," Ginger suggested, "and I'll head them off."

Billy lifted his smoothly shaven chin when they claimed two empty stools. "What's your poison?" he asked Basil.

"Another whisky," Basil said.

Ginger giggled. "*Moi, aussi.* Me, too." Anything the dancers ordered from the bar came off their pay, and Billy duly made note.

Basil noticed too. "I'll pay for hers."

Billy was quick to pour their drinks, and Ginger lifted her glass to Basil. "To whatever comes next."

He held her gaze and clinked her glass.

"So, Billy," Ginger called, leaning over the bar. The barman settled his ocean-blue eyes on her in a way that made Ginger shiver. "Did you hear that Cindy was arrested backstage?"

The smile fell off the barman's face. "Word is spreading from table to table. If she did it, she deserves to hang."

"Oh, *mon ami*. Do you think she did it?"

Billy shrugged.

"Did you know the dancer who died?" Basil asked casually. "Was she popular?"

Billy snorted. "You could say that again. There's not a man here who didn't scramble for her attention."

Basil swallowed hard. "Did *you* scramble for her attention?"

"I wouldn't be a man if I hadn't," Billy said stiffly. "Destiny was enigmatic. Not like these other girls who are ten a penny." He glanced at Ginger. "Present company excluded, of course."

"Did you see her the night she died?" Ginger said, adding quickly "I just can't believe no one saw anything."

Billy dried a glass and shrugged. "Last I saw her she was leaving the club—just as alive as you and me." The barman turned abruptly to serve other patrons.

"What's his name?" Basil asked quietly.

"Billy Foster. Are you going to get your constable to see what he can find out about him?"

Basil raised a brow. "It would seem prudent."

"Antoinette!" Nuala sidled up beside Basil. "No keeping this handsome man to yourself." She giggled and pressed up against Basil in a way Ginger didn't like. Nuala held out a dainty hand. "I'm Nuala."

Basil accepted her hand and held it to his lips. "It's a pleasure to meet you Miss Nuala. I'm Archie."

Ginger straightened in surprise at this nom de plume. *Archie*? Where did *that* come from?

"Oh, Archie, such a gentleman calling me, miss." Nuala positioned herself between Basil and Ginger. She whispered sharply in Ginger's ear. "Spread yourself out. Conway doesn't like it when one man dominates unless he's paying."

"I see someone I must say hello to," Ginger said above the din of the club. She finger-waved over her shoulder and fluttered her eyelashes in a flirtatious manner. "Au revoir, *Archie*."

Conway Sayer stood at his usual position at the club entrance. From that position, he could watch the door, the stage, and the bar. Ginger sashayed his way. "Monsieur Sayer, I'm afraid I'm in need of the *toilette*."

"That's why I tell you not to drink after the show," he said without empathy.

"Sometimes, nature calls. It cannot be helped."

"Go then, but be quick about it."

Ginger moseyed away, but as soon as she was out of Conway's line of sight, she hurried to the manager's office. There were plenty of pins in her wig to do the trick of picking the lock, and Ginger was inside in no time.

The office was impeccably tidy, a stark contrast to the girls' changing room. There was a filing cabinet, a desk and chair, even a plant, which, miraculously was still alive given the window faced north and the natural lighting was minimal. The linoleum on the floor was scuffed but swept clean. A broom was tucked away behind the door. There wasn't even a water ring on the wooden desk, not a crumb from a sandwich eaten while working.

Ginger struck gold in the top drawer of the desk. A ledger lay inside which she could flip through without removing. As the club manager, Conway Sayer tracked the funds. Ginger flipped through the few pages looking for anything amiss. Nothing. Underneath that ledger were three others. Ginger slipped the latest one out and pushed it down her girdle.

A further search through the drawers delivered her answer. Italian mafia boss, Charles Sabini. Ginger groaned. Did that man own all the clubs in London?

Ginger was familiar with the extent of Sabini's reach as she had encountered his drug operation not long before. She quickly closed the desk drawers, ensuring that everything was left exactly as she had found it, right down to the inch. She had to hurry back before Sayer decided to look for her.

The manager scowled at her suspiciously when she returned. "Took you long enough."

Ginger giggled demurely. "*C'est la vie.*"

It was Ginger's turn to scowl when she saw Nuala practically pinning Basil to the bar. She forced herself not to stare and made her way to Haley and Felicia. Fortunately, Mr. Phillips had left.

"How are you holding up?" Haley asked.

"This life is exhausting!" Ginger said.

Haley pushed her drink to her friend. "It's Coca-Cola."

"A little cocaine to wake me up," Ginger said taking

a sip. "Did you learn anything new from our friend Mr. Phillips?"

"He's a churlish beast," Felicia said indignantly. "When I refused him, he left us, said we were a waste of time."

"He did leave us with a little tidbit," Haley said.

Felicia stared back at Haley with a look of surprise. "He did?"

"When we brought up the subject of Cindy's arrest, I overheard Mr. Phillips mutter.

"What did he say?" Felicia demanded, looking put out that she'd missed a potential clue.

"Yes," Ginger added. "What did he say?"

"*That's what happens to women who don't know their place,*" Haley replied.

"Oh, mercy," Ginger said. "That sounds antagonistic, not to mention misogynistic."

"My guess is that Emelia Reed crossed a personal line," Haley said.

Ginger agreed. "What line exactly?"

Felicia's attention tuned in to something happening over Ginger's shoulder. Ginger turned and frowned. Nuala was persistent if nothing else. She was pulling on Basil's arm, intent on taking him somewhere.

Haley shoved her chair back and stood. "I'll pretend to be his sister."

"Good idea. Don't forget to alter your accent," Ginger said, grateful for Haley's ability to think on her feet. She called after her just in time. "His name is Archie!"

CHAPTER TWENTY-ONE

A fast rapping on Ginger's bedroom door pulled her from a deep sleep. She'd been dreaming about the storm she and Haley had experienced on the SS *Rosa* when they crossed the Atlantic the previous summer. The sudden and fierce storm had drenched Ginger as she struggled to make it to her stateroom, the deck slippery and uneven as the ship lurched. She fell, bruised her elbows and knees as she slid to the rail, hanging on . . .

An urgent whisper called out. "Lady Gold!"

Boss answered with a short "yip."

Ginger propped up on one elbow, willing her heart to slow. The dream wasn't real, but the rain pounded so hard it sounded like someone was throwing sand against the windows. "Who is it?"

"Matilda. Please, help me."

Ginger jumped out of bed, grabbed her blue silk

negligée and slipped it over a matching camisole and bloomers ensemble.

On the other side of the door stood Matilda Hanson, her face a ghostly white. Her eyes rolled back as she slumped, and Ginger barely caught her before Matilda fell to the floor.

"Haley!" Ginger yelled out. "Haley!"

Haley's bedroom door opened, and she flicked on the electric lights. "What's wrong?" Then on seeing Ginger holding Matilda, "Miss Hanson?"

"She's fainted," Ginger said. "Oh, no." With the lights on, she could see a vast stain of blood on the midsection of Matilda's night clothes.

Haley saw it too. "Let's get her back in her bed."

Ambrosia stood at her door, grey hair peeking out of a night cap, her silk dressing gown wrapped tightly around a soft body. "What on earth is going on?"

"Grandmother, go and tell Felicia to call for a doctor," Ginger instructed. "Then summon Lizzie and Grace."

Ambrosia stared with a disbelieving expression as Ginger and Haley awkwardly carried Matilda. The blood stain was obvious.

"Grandmother! It's an emergency!"

Ambrosia snapped out of her trance and yelled for Felicia. She tapped her walking stick down the hall while muttering, "The child could sleep through the Second Coming," then used it to knock loudly on Felicia's door.

Ginger was out of breath when they finally had

Matilda lying down. She focused on the rising of Matilda's chest. Her breathing was faint, but there. Her pale skin was clammy to the touch. "What's happening?"

"She's miscarrying," Haley said. "She's in shock."

Ginger's heart lurched. Miss Hanson was nearly six months along.

"We'll have to remove her clothing," Haley said, already in the process. "Giving birth is not the most dignified thing in the world."

"And the poor thing won't even have a live babe as a reward." Ginger's heart went out to her new friend. She felt terrible for the disappointed family Oliver had lined up for adoption. She'd once had to deliver a baby in France, but that one had had a happy ending.

"We have to work quickly," Haley said, "before she loses too much blood."

An uproar in the hallway led to the arrival of Felicia and the maids.

"Dear Lord," Felicia said at the sight of all the blood. "Is she dead?"

"No," Haley said. "We need hot water, clean towels, and water for Miss Hanson to drink. And a bucket!"

Felicia instructed Lizzie and Grace to get the requested items and to hurry.

"You should dress," Ginger said to Felicia, "then wait for the doctor to arrive."

"The telephone lines are down," Felicia said, her voice pitched high. "Should I send Clement?"

"Yes," Ginger said. "Do it now."

Lizzie arrived with the bucket then hurried away.

Matilda moaned in pain as her body convulsed.

"Miss Hanson," Haley said, shouting in Matilda's ear. "You have to wake up. It's time to push."

Matilda moaned but seemed far away. Haley slapped her face. "Matilda!"

Matilda's eyes rounded, glassy with pain, as the next contraction hit.

"Push!"

"It's too soon!" Matilda pleaded.

Ginger held Matilda's hand tightly. "You have to push, love."

Haley glanced at Ginger, her worried eyes saying the worst. If the baby wasn't born soon, the mother might die as well.

Matilda yelled with shiver-inducing agony, doing her bit, and a perfect little boy, the size of Ginger's palm, was born.

Everyone knew the baby was dead, and Matilda burst into tears. Ginger felt her own eyes burn with grief and shared a tear.

Matilda collapsed with exhaustion.

"Have a drink of water," Ginger said. "You've lost a lot of blood." If Haley hadn't been there to deliver the baby, they could be mourning the death of two people instead of one. Ginger held Matilda's head as she drank.

Felicia hovered by the door. "It's over?"

Haley nodded. "Yes."

"The doctor is here."

Dr. Longden, a familiar figure to Hartigan House, was a capable physician getting close to his retirement years. Ginger had full confidence in his abilities, but she was unable to relax until the man had examined Matilda and reassured Ginger that the patient was stable. She would need a lot of rest for the next few days. Haley offered to stay with Matilda for the rest of the night, which comforted Ginger. Matilda would be too weak to call out or to help herself should she need assistance.

Ginger urged everyone to get back to bed and crawled into her own large bed with Boss at her side. "Such a sad turn of events," Ginger said softly as she found comfort in her pet's warm form. "Thankfully, we still have Miss Hanson with us."

With the dramatic event behind them, Ginger tossed and turned, rather than slept. She forced herself to think of something other than the night's tragedy, and her mind went to the murder case, and specifically Conway Sayer.

Ginger couldn't put her finger on it, but something about the man, other than his obvious disdain of women, made her feel ill at ease.

"Move over, Bossy," she said as she crawled out of bed for the second time that night. She turned on the electric lamp on her bedside table and removed Conway's ledger from her costume bag. She puffed up her pillow against the engraved headboard before climbing back in.

Turning the pages, Ginger examined the entries, not sure what she was looking for or hoped to find. There was a row of money coming in, liquor sales mostly, and several for money going out: alcohol, utilities, cleaning and maintenance services, and wages for the dancers. Ginger choked on the meagre amount and muttered, "Cheapskate." At least the girls got to keep their tips.

She watched for patterns, similarities from month to month. She flipped from the end of 1923 to the beginning of 1924 and noticed an anomaly.

It wasn't overly large, just a slight change in the amount coming in, a drop in five pounds a week, but that went up to seven pounds in February and ten pounds in March.

Conway Sayer was pilfering funds. Had Emelia Reed found out? Did Conway kill her to keep her quiet?

GINGER MET Basil at a Regent Street tea room. It was just like old times when Basil was getting a divorce instead of planning a funeral. She wore a copper-colored rayon day dress with bell sleeves, a contrasting lace collar, and a drop-waist skirt with four-panel layers that stopped mid-calf. She paired her dress with black, two-inch pumps and a white broad-brimmed hat pulled low on her forehead.

Basil wore a pinstriped suit, a crisply pressed shirt with black tie, and polished leather shoes. She ordered piping hot coffee with a biscuit and he, a pot of tea and a crumpet.

"We had an eventful night," Ginger said, then filled him in on Matilda Hanson's sad news. "Haley said the baby had been dead for a couple of weeks or so."

"How awful. But I suppose Matilda can get back to her studies now."

"The spring term's over, Basil. She has to wait until autumn."

"Of course. I'm sorry. My mind isn't . . ."

"It's fine," Ginger said. Basil hadn't been the same since he'd lost both Emilia and access to his job. His wasn't the only loss, but Ginger wouldn't stoop so low to compare hers to his.

"What is she going to do now?" he asked.

"She can stay with me," Ginger said after a bite of her chocolate biscuit. "But, I suppose she no longer has to remain housebound."

"It'll be good for her to get outside."

Ginger stared at Basil. Their conversation had become bland and boring. "Yes, a little sun is what she needs."

Over the last three months, she and Basil had seen each other nearly every day and never once had they lacked for inspiring conversation. Now Basil just stared into his tea.

"I think I'm going to go," Ginger said.

"No," Basil's head snapped up. "Please, I'm sorry. I'm just trying to make sense of things, and blast, it's difficult."

Ginger relented. "Maybe I can help you. What's the first thing that doesn't make sense?"

His gaze locked onto hers and he swallowed. "It's spectacularly unfair of me to discuss her with you."

"But we must," Ginger said. "Surely, you realize that?"

Basil sighed. "We were happy once. Then the war happened. And even though I wasn't away that long, it was long enough . . ."

For Emelia to find comfort in the arms of other men.

"She always was a wild sort. Bucked against societal restraints. She had a strict upbringing. Her mother's efforts to control her were extreme, suffocating, really. I don't know why I thought I could tame her. I think she married me simply to get out from under her parents' rule."

Ginger didn't know what to say to this. She sipped her coffee and muttered, "I see."

"I had no idea that she spent her free time at clubs—she was nothing more than an exhibitionist."

"Well, there is maybe something more to it than that."

Basil's head snapped up. "Like what?"

"With all the rules and expectations put on young ladies in proper society, a place like that allows one the freedom to be what one wants. It's why Felicia and her friends like to go there."

"To smoke and drink," Basil said, "but to take off

your clothes? In front of a room full of leering men? I'm sorry, I can't accept that."

"No one's asking you to. Don't get me wrong. I don't think it's an ideal environment. It can certainly be dangerous. And for the record, I don't enjoy making a spectacle of myself for the pleasure of lustful men. I find it belittling. I just don't think we can sit here and judge. There's more to these girls stories than what meets the eye."

"I don't want you to go back there."

Ginger blinked thick lashes. "But the case?"

"We've already found out everything we're going to at the North Star."

"Oh, really?" Ginger sat back and folded her arms.

"Really."

"I don't agree. Conway Sayer is pilfering." Ginger filled him in on Conway's ledger. "I think Emelia found out."

"You nicked Conway Sayer's ledger?"

"I *borrowed* it."

Basil scowled at that, then leaned in. "Even if Emelia did discover this, you can't prove it."

"Not yet. That's why I have to go back. Besides, you asked me to help."

"I'm *unasking* you."

"Unasking is not a word."

"I'm asking you not to Ginger. It's getting danger-ous. I couldn't live with myself if I lost you both."

Lost you both.

Basil's words stretched between them like a

tightrope. Ginger remembered the circus act her father had taken her to see in Boston. Massive white tents topped with little flags, colorful signs, and unique-looking people inviting the crowds inside. Father had bought her salty popcorn and sweet toffee.

Zebras were treated like horses, and elephants did incredible tricks. She remembered one that balanced its front two legs on the top of wine bottles!

The high-wire walkers had made her little heart stop. The most beautiful woman she had ever seen balanced gracefully high above her head. The spectators held their breath as if by the pure power of their combined will they would propel the acrobat to safety.

Then she fell. Oxygen escaped the room, first with deafening silence and then deafening pandemonium, until the lady presented herself unharmed, bouncing to the ground from the net that had saved her life. The tension in the tent had turned from hard to soft, hot to cold. Screams to giddy laughter.

Just like this moment.

"You won't lose me," Ginger finally said. "I have my pistol, which I'll keep in my garter at all times. Besides," she added with a lightness she didn't feel. "You'll be there to protect me. I couldn't be safer."

Basil breathed heavily through his nose. "You are the most stubborn woman on the planet."

Ginger smiled and lifted her coffee cup. "Thank you. I think we should visit the Johnson Building. It's where the dancers live."

"All of them?"

"They get a bit of a deal since it's owned by the club owner." Ginger checked her slim, diamond-encrusted watch. "They'll be heading to the club soon. We'd have time to take a peek before I need to head over there."

Basil shook his head but didn't bother arguing. He paid the cashier before they left.

CHAPTER TWENTY-TWO

*C*ross from the Johnson Building that afternoon, Ginger and Basil waited in Ginger's Crossley. Basil agreed on taking her motorcar since Ginger had her Antoinette wig and dance costume in her boot, and she'd only have enough time to snoop through the girls' flats before heading to the club. She didn't want to get on Conway's wrong side by being late.

"How are we going to get in without a key?" Basil asked.

Ginger tapped her hat. "I don't really need hat pins to keep this style in place, but one never knows when one will be in need of hat pins."

Nuala and Sorcha stepped out of the building. Automatically, Ginger and Basil slunk low in the leather seats. The dancers headed in the opposite direction from where Ginger had purposely parked.

Picking open the door to a flat was one thing, but the entrance door to the building was quite another. Ginger and Basil loitered by the front door, and before long a resident left, and Basil caught the door just before it latched closed. The building needed paint and smelled slightly of mould and lingering cigarette smoke. In the lobby, Ginger checked the copper-plated post boxes, but none were listed with the names Nuala and Sorcha—obviously fake names. Only last names were listed on the boxes, so it was impossible to tell male residents from female. However, she spotted the name C. Webb on one post box.

"Cindy's in two o nine. Can't tell with the others." She searched for B. Foster but came up empty. "They said Billy Foster was in this building, but I don't see his name? Do you?"

Basil shook his head. "A. Chatwyn, S. Haley, W. Phillips, J. Stanley, B. Hackman."

Ginger and Basil headed up to the next floor, and as providence would have it, the caretaker was leaving with a bag of rubbish in hand.

"Excuse us, sir," Ginger said. "We've promised our friends we'd come and visit today, but they neglected to give us their flat number. They're flatmates, one brunette and one blonde."

"Yes, I know them," he said. "Nice girls. Room two o six."

Fortunately, the man hadn't seen Nuala and Sorcha leave. Ginger smiled and said, "Thank you, kindly."

They waited until the passageway was quiet.

"Which one first?" Ginger asked.

Basil pointed. "Two o six is right here."

Ginger glanced to her right and saw the numbers on the door. Even though she was wearing gloves, she refrained from touching the railing. The caretaker might tend to the rubbish, but from the sticky look of the banisters, he didn't care about much else.

The cry of a baby filtered out from the flat next door, but the passageway was empty. Ginger used her hat pins to disengage the lock mechanism and slipped inside.

"This is breaking and entering," Basil said unable to hide his note of disapproval.

Ginger shot him a look. "Are you going to call the police?"

Basil snorted and followed her inside.

The flat looked like a bomb had gone off. Clothes flung everywhere, a stained sofa and a scratched-up matching chair. An overfull ashtray littered the table along with dirty glasses and bottles of beer. A small dish on the floor in the corner appeared to be the dried remnants of cat food. The kitchen tap dripped every three seconds.

"That would drive me crazy," Basil said.

"This mess would drive me crazy," Ginger said. "How do they manage to find anything?

Basil disappeared into the shared bedroom while Ginger opened kitchen drawers. At least the ones that weren't already balancing half-open. They searched for something that might link either woman to Emelia Reed and Cindy's snake.

Ginger spotted a photo leaning against the windowsill. She picked it up to take a closer look. It was a blurry image of a woman and a man sitting close to each other. The light-haired woman was Sorcha, but Ginger had to squint to make out the man. Billy Foster?

Ginger jumped when a dish fell into the sink, and her hand sprang to her heart. The owner of the cat food bowl meowed and narrowed accusing yellow eyes.

Basil raced into the kitchen. "Are you all right?"

"It's just the cat. Came up out of nowhere." Ginger handed Basil the photograph. "Cindy said Sorcha was soft on Billy Foster who was . . ." Ginger hesitated. Talking about Emelia's reckless and disloyal lifestyle with Basil would never be easy. Billy and Destiny had . . ."

"It's fine, Ginger. I get it."

"Right. Well, perhaps Sorcha's obsession drove her to kill off her competition? I suspect Sorcha is more intelligent than she leads everyone to believe."

"Women usually are," Basil muttered.

Ginger ignored the comment. "But, would Sorcha dare to handle Cindy's snake?"

Leaving everything just as they found it, they locked 206 behind them and quietly entered 209.

The layout of Cynthia Webb's flat was a mirror image of Nuala's and Sorcha's, and unlike the flatmates, Cindy liked to keep her environment tidy and organized. There was little in the way of furniture, just a small table, two chairs, and in the bedroom, a mattress on the floor.

"I don't see any reptiles," Ginger said. A cardboard box rested on the ground beside the bed. Ginger lifted the flaps. "This is interesting." She raised a glass jar. "*Jeune et Belle* face cream. I saw Sorcha using this at the club." Ginger replaced the jar and did a quick count. "There's a dozen jars in this box."

Basil stood in front of the wardrobe. "There's another three boxes in here."

"What is she doing with it, I wonder?" Ginger said. She sniffed the cream before twisting the lid back on. It smelled like Emelia, but she didn't say it out loud.

Back in the kitchen, Basil opened the door of the ice box. It was small but large enough to hold a bottle of milk and a couple of dead mice. "Snake food," Basil said. Ginger felt slightly nauseous at the sight.

Near the entrance, an empty reptile cage attracted a small swarm of black flies.

"If Cindy had a poisonous snake," Basil said, "she may have disposed of it already."

"We could check the bins out the back."

Basil agreed it would be the appropriate thing to do, and a precise but unpleasant search produced only what one would expect. No dead snakes.

"I'm going to go back to the club from here as Antoinette," Ginger announced when they were back in her Crossley.

"I'll go with you."

"You can't come in. It's too early."

"I just want to make sure you get inside all right."

Ginger relented. "Why don't you drive, and I'll get ready." She handed Basil the keys. He started the motorcar and pulled into the traffic while Ginger pinned her hair back and donned the Antoinette wig. She could dress in her costume at the club.

"I'll take a taxicab back to Mayfair," Basil said after parking the Crossley. "I'll meet you here tonight."

Ginger smiled back at Basil's grim countenance. "It's a plan." However, she encountered a snag at the back entrance. Conway Sayer had been watching for her.

"Take the night off," he said gruffly. "I don't need you."

"But with Cindy gone?" Ginger sputtered with her French accent.

"I'm trying out new girls tonight. Come back tomorrow."

"But, Mr. Sayer—"

"Tomorrow." He shut the door in her face.

Thankfully, Basil had yet to flag down a taxicab, and he looked at Ginger in surprise when she, with her blonde wig, approached.

"Apparently, it's my day off," she said. "I'm not sure if I've been sacked or not."

"A fly in the ointment."

Ginger worked her lips in thought. "I think I know a way to remove it."

CHAPTER TWENTY-THREE

*G*inger heard someone walking down the passageway at Hartigan House, and when she peeked out, she was glad to see Haley. She waved Haley into her bedroom.

"What do you think?" Ginger said, patting at her new dark hair do, shorter than how she normally wore it. "Lizzie procured me the wig."

"Who are you now?" Haley asked, her dark eyes flashing with amusement.

"Georgia."

"Your given name?"

Because Ginger had been born with a mass of ginger-colored hair, Ginger's mother had given baby Georgia the nickname.

"Georgia hardly gets used," Ginger said. "I thought it was time I took it out for a spin."

"Dare I ask, *Georgia*, to what end?" Haley said.

LEE STRAUSS

"I'm going out on a date."

Haley ducked her chin. "As Georgia?"

"Yes, well, it's Basil taking me."

Haley's dark brow arched high, a signature look when she found something unusual, amusing, or questionable. "And he wants to call you Georgia now?"

"No, that's my cover."

"Wait. Basil's taking you out to the North Star Club?"

Ginger nodded. She slipped into a dark grey sleeveless dress exquisitely embroidered with shiny silver thread. A six-inch fringe in the style of lampshade trim hung below the under slip, allowing for tantalizing glimpses of her stockinged legs from the knee.

Haley's forehead wrinkled with confusion. "But, they know you there as Antoinette?"

"It's Antoinette's night off. Would you mind buttoning me up?"

"You're not making any sense." Haley deftly worked the buttons, and Ginger selected a pair of black satin André Perugia shoes.

"I am." Ginger added a jeweled headpiece with a string of rhinestones that looped along her forehead with a fluffy red feather at her temple. "Conway Sayer won't pay any attention to 'Georgia.'" She twirled, and the fringe of her dress billowed. "Dressed like this, I'll blend in with all the other flapper girls."

Haley tucked her curls into her faux bob. "I'm coming."

"But Basil . . ."

"Don't worry. I won't be your third wheel. I'll bring Felicia, and we'll take a taxicab."

Ginger grinned. She would feel better if they were there to watch her back.

"Fabulous."

BASIL PICKED her up in his Austin 7. He looked *très debonair* in his tailored suit and trilby hat.

"I could've met you there," Ginger said, pushing aside the emotions that stirred at the sight of him. "Haley and Felicia are coming later by taxicab."

Basil opened the passenger door. "It's my pleasure to pick you up, Ginger," he said, holding her gloved hand as she relaxed into the seat. "This way I get some time alone with you."

Ginger valued the time alone as well, but the distance passed by in silence. It was like they were strangers, meeting for the first time."

"It's a nice evening," Ginger offered. "I love the smell of spring in the air."

"Yes," Basil said.

"What do you think of my new look?" Ginger asked. "You didn't say."

"I'm assuming it's so your pals at the club don't recognize you as Antoinette."

"Yes, but do you like it?"

"Yes. Although, I prefer your natural hair color."

"I'm going as 'Georgia' should anyone ask."

Basil merely nodded. Ginger waited for him to say

more, engage in a bout of flirtatious banter, verbal acrobatics they were both skilled at.

"I heard from my man at the Yard," Basil said. "Cynthia Webb's been released due to lack of evidence."

"That doesn't mean she's not guilty."

"Agreed."

A long pause thickened between them.

"When is the funeral?" Ginger finally said. She thought she might as well ask. Emelia was present with them again, anyway. She could almost feel her displeased spirit.

Basil changed gears. "I don't know. The inquest is tomorrow."

"Would you like me to come with you?"

"I think it would be best if I go alone."

"Oh."

"It's just that her parents will be there."

"I understand." And she did, yet somehow, she still felt discarded. "You have your in-laws to think about."

Basil glanced at her sideways. "We don't always have to talk about her."

"It seems to be the only thing *to* talk about."

Basil sighed. "Maybe you're right. Until this case is solved."

Ginger swallowed. What if it was never solved?

BASIL LED her to the darkest corner table in the back of the room. Conway Sayer never gave her a second glance, but Billy wasn't so easily fooled. Ginger felt his eyes on her as her fringed hem shimmied against her knees. She'd barely been seated when Billy came to the table himself to ask for their drinks order.

"Antoinette?" Billy said with a smirk, "or are you using another alias tonight?"

"Billy!" Ginger said, now with an American accent. "You are a brute!" She pulled out an ivory cigarette holder and shot a look at Basil. He recovered from his moment of shock—Ginger had never lit up in his presence before—and produced a cigarette and lighter.

Billy chuckled. "You're American."

"Yup. Just having a bit of fun while I'm visiting London." She looked up at him from under heavily mascaraed eyelashes. "I trust you won't give me away."

"Not my business. Can I get the two of you something to drink? Whiskies again?"

Ginger pulled on her cigarette and blew smoke out from the side of her mouth. She'd smoked in France as part of a cover once, but that had been a long time ago. She was thankful she didn't erupt in a fit of coughing. "Gin and tonic," she said. She hated being predictable.

"I'll have that too," Basil added.

Haley and Felicia arrived and claimed a table in the middle of the room. If they saw Ginger there they didn't make a show of it. Ginger was impressed at the intuitive judge of character and situation they each seemed to have.

A couple made an entrance, a young girl on the arm of a man twice her age. She was rosy-cheeked with dark shadow and heavy mascara on eager eyes. She looked familiar but so altered, Ginger had to do a second take.

"*Oh, mercy.*"

Basil followed her gaze. "What is it? Do you know them?"

"I don't know him. Her I know. It's Dorothy West! My shop assistant."

"You seem surprised."

"I *am*. My goodness, talk about a double life."

"I take it she's much different from the lady I'm looking at now."

"Dorothy is self-conscious and self-deprecating. Innocent and demure. She's soft on the vicar, for pity's sake."

Basil snorted. "I doubt that she's innocent. The question is, did she know Emelia?"

Mr. Jonathon Phillips strutted in, stopping to chat with Conway Sayer who kept to his position near the entrance.

"There's John Phillips," Ginger said with a nod. The middle-aged man was having words with Conway Sayer, and it didn't appear to be a pleasant conversation. "I'm going over there."

Ginger bounded out of her seat before Basil could stop her, ignoring his plea for her to wait. She called over her shoulder, "I won't be long."

Conway turned in a huff before Ginger could position herself to eavesdrop. Mr. Phillips smiled when he saw her, and she was happy to note that his oh-so-blue eyes hadn't flashed with recognition.

"Georgia," Ginger said with an American drawl.

He dipped his head and accepted her gloved hand, raising it to his lips. "Jonathon Phillips. It's a pleasure."

"Would you be interested . . ." She pronounced it *inneresded*.". . . in buying a girl a drink?"

Phillips' eyes sparkled. "Absolutely."

Ginger ordered a whisky, but only played with a drop on her tongue. She needed to keep her head.

"What part of America are you from?" Phillips asked.

"New York."

"Fantastic city."

"You've been?"

"A couple of times. Business."

Ginger knew not to ask what kind of business. The "rule of thumb" in *this* business was to stay clear of personal questions.

"How about you?" Ginger asked. "You sound southern."

John Phillips smiled. "Virginia."

"Never been, but hear it's lovely." Ginger watched the man from under heavily made-up eyes. "What brings you to London?"

"Business. You?"

She smiled flirtatiously. "Adventure."

John Phillips' eyes narrowed though remained friendly. "Have I seen you here before? You look familiar."

"I don't think so. I refused to patronize the North

Star as long as that tart—" Ginger made a face—"Destiny, came here."

"Ah. I take it you weren't friends."

"That woman was nobody's friend. The most selfish pill I'd ever met. Would you believe she tried to *blackmail* me?"

Ginger kept her eyes on Phillips, gauging his reaction carefully. He tried to hide his response, but she saw it in the flicker of his eyelashes and the tensing of his jaw.

"Oh, forgive me!" Ginger said. "You *knew* her, I suppose. I'm such a dunce."

Phillips knocked back the rest of his whisky and ordered another. "I knew her. I'm sure every man in this room did."

Ginger couldn't help but glance at Basil.

The alcohol had loosened Phillips' tongue. "You're not the only one Destiny tried to blackmail, so don't feel bad."

"Really? *You?* That snake. I hate her even more now."

Ginger had to remind herself that she was playing a part. Emelia was dead, and Ginger was resolute in her determination to remain charitable.

"Well, she's gone now," Phillips said with no hint of remorse. "Now, hey, wait a minute." His eyes rounded as realization dawned. "You're Antoinette!"

Ginger figured this would happen eventually and was prepared. She giggled and reverted to her French accent and patted his arm. "I had you fooled,

Monsieur!" Going back to her American accent, "Or do you prefer an American girl."

Mr. Phillip's lips pulled up slyly. "Join me at my table, and I'll think about it." Ginger linked her arm with his and, her long, seductive fringe swaying, she sashayed to the diplomat's table, once again feeling the heat of Basil's glare on her back.

When she passed Felicia and Haley, she put on another show. "Hello, ladies! Look who I'm with this fine evenin'. Ain't he the most handsome man you ever did see?"

Felicia's jaw dropped at Ginger's personality trans-formation, but Haley had grown accustomed to Ginger's American accent in Boston—though Ginger was undoubtedly more reserved than Georgia!

Mr. Phillips' table was closer to the piano, and the louder music forced her to have to lean in to listen to him. Phillips offered her a cigarette, and Ginger accepted.

He chuckled as he watched her. "You really should be in the pictures."

"Why do ya say that?"

"Well, you're a chameleon. Do Antoinette again!"

Ginger put her cigarette down, cupped her hands and placed them under her chin and spoke French. "*Les secrets d'une fille sont les siennes.*"

Phillips' head fell back as he laughed. "All that's missing is the blonde hair."

He leaned closer, and Ginger felt the man's warm

breath on her cheek. "Who are you really? Georgia, the brunette?"

Ginger tilted her head back and smiled wryly. "Who are *you*, really?"

"Ha," Phillips said. "As you French like to say, *touché*."

Ginger checked her watch. The show would start shortly, and Ginger was curious who these new dancers were. It seemed there was no shortage of women willing to parade themselves, whether out of desperation or, as in Emelia's case—and apparently Dorothy West's—diversion.

Ginger watched Dorothy out of the corner of her eye. The man she was with looked as if he would devour the girl, and Ginger wondered if Dorothy *really* knew what she was getting herself into.

Phillips had followed her gaze. Apparently, he knew the man and waved them over.

Oh, mercy.

"Richard Price, my good man," Phillips bellowed. "Bring your pretty lady, and come join us."

It was amazing how hair and makeup could confuse a person of one's identity if one wasn't well acquainted. However, Dorothy knew Ginger's face.

Dorothy was too busy swooning over Mr. Price to notice at first, but once seated, Phillips made introductions.

"This is Georgia." Dorothy automatically held out her hand, and Ginger took it, catching her young floor clerk's eyes. "Nice to meet you," Ginger said. Her accent was

American, but Dorothy knew her true identity immediately. The flush of excitement from Dorothy's face drained to white as the reality of her situation settled in.

Dorothy withdrew her hand and clasped it to her mouth. She yelped and rushed from the table toward the ladies' room.

"She must've eaten something off," Ginger said. "It can come upon you all of a sudden, like. I bet she ate shellfish. Nasty stuff." Ginger butted out her cigarette. "I'll go see to the poor thing."

Ginger found Dorothy clinging to the porcelain sink, mascara running down her cheeks. When she caught Ginger's reflection in the mirror, the girl stared back as if she had seen a ghost.

"Oh, L—"

Ginger shook her head sharply and put a finger to her lips. She could see a pair of T-strap shoes under one of the cubicle doors.

"You ate some bad fish, didn't you?" Ginger said, keeping her American persona intact. "I've sworn off the stuff. My mother made us eat it every Friday—and we're not even Catholic! Said it was good for us or some crazy thing."

The toilet flushed, and a young lady dressed in full flapper mode stood beside a stunned Dorothy and washed her hands. "You definitely don't look well, love," she commiserated. As soon as she had left, Ginger quickly locked the door.

"Lady Gold? I'm so embarrassed. *Mortified.*"

"What are you doing, Dorothy?" Ginger returned to her natural accent. "That man has intentions."

"I know, I don't know," Dorothy whined miserably. "I was just curious. My life is so dull, and men never pay attention to me, that was until I met—"

Ginger lowered her chin. "Met Emelia Reed?"

"Yes. She was handing pamphlets out on women's health. She said so I could protect myself." Dorothy's neck flushed red. "I don't know. I was just curious! This isn't me, really!"

"How many times have you been to this club?"

"Only a few, with Mrs. Reed. She said she'd help break me out of my shell. That she could show me how to really live life!"

"And now she's dead," Ginger said pointedly.

"Oh, I know. I'm such a stupid girl."

Ginger studied her floor clerk, feeling unnerved and, dare she admit, suspicious. Dorothy was acting the young innocent, but her behavior with Mr. Price looked sincere. But then again, Ginger hoped her performance was as believable.

"Establishments like this are not meant for nice girls like you, Dorothy," Ginger said kindly. "Unsavory activities take place here."

Dorothy stared at Ginger with bloodshot eyes. "Why are *you* here, Lady Gold?"

"I'm investigating Emelia Reed's murder."

"Oh."

"How did Mrs. Reed come to be in possession of your grandmother's hair clip?"

Dorothy's shoulders slumped. "She admired it so openly, I felt compelled to offer to lend it to her."

Why was Emelia grasping the clip when she died? Perhaps it was nothing more than the clip coming loose and Emelia holding on to it.

"Now," Ginger said, feeling very matronly, "clean yourself up, and we'll take you home."

"Who's we?"

"Me and Chief Inspector Reed."

Dorothy's stricken look returned. "Oh, no, I couldn't. I was privy to his wife's philandering. Aided and abetted, you could say." A new terrible thought occurred to her, and she blurted out, "Oh! Lady Gold. You won't tell Reverend Hill, will you?"

Ginger stared hard at Dorothy. "I don't see why I should, so long as you promise never to behave in such a dangerous and reckless manner again."

"I promise, I do." Dorothy wiped her face with her handkerchief. "I'll take a taxicab home."

"I'll tell Mr. Price you're too ill to stay."

Dorothy stood before Ginger looking sheepish. "Thank you, Lady Gold. Er, do you still want me to come into work this week."

"Of course. I'm short-staffed as it is." Ginger had thought about employing another girl more than once. "And it's not like you broke the law . . . and if you did," Ginger held up a palm," . . . don't tell me!"

That elicited a half-smile. "Thank you, madam."

An angry knock on the door ended their conversation. "So, sorry," Ginger said, back to her American persona. "The door accidentally jammed shut."

Ginger delivered her message to Mr. Price, who frowned. "Ungrateful girl."

"I'm afraid I have to say goodbye, too, Mr. Phillips."

The man grabbed her roughly by the arm. "We're not done."

Ginger saw Basil jump to his feet. Haley and Felicia had tensed as well.

As quick as lightning, Ginger swung her free fist under the man's arm and hammered his elbow. He cried out in pain.

"I'm so sorry, Mr. Phillips," Ginger said. "I lost my footing there." She stepped back out of arm's reach. "As I was about to say. I came with someone else. An amateur boxer." She waved at Basil who was headed her way. "See, there he is."

Mr. Phillips muttered threatening words. He was an abusive bully, and Emelia had crossed him. Ginger had to watch herself. The diplomat could very well be a killer.

CHAPTER TWENTY-FOUR

*T*he next day, after calling in at Feathers & Flair and being reassured by Madame Roux that she had everything under control, Ginger returned to Hartigan House to find Haley and Felicia drinking tea in the sitting room.

"I'll get Lizzie to make you a fresh pot," Felicia said. Her temperament over these last few days had improved from her usual unpredictable sensitivity. Perhaps she'd finally moved on from her moody adolescence.

Ginger collapsed into her chair, and Boss, who'd followed her in with his bounty of unconditional love, jumped on her lap and stuck a wet nose against her neck.

"Oh, Bossy," Ginger cooed. "I missed you too."

Pats and strokes calmed the small animal, and his body relaxed into a ball.

"You're home already?" Ginger said to Haley. She checked her watch. "It's barely noon. And here I was beginning to think they'd put a bed up in the mortuary for you."

Haley stretched out an arm and then suppressed a yawn. "No. I get this afternoon and all of tomorrow off."

"Brilliant. Do you have plans?"

"My usual. Sleep and read, then sleep some more."

Felicia returned with Lizzie on her heels. "Here's some fresh tea for you, madam," the young maid said. She poured Ginger a cup, added half a teaspoon of sugar, and stirred it before placing it on a matching saucer and handing it to Ginger.

"Thank you, Lizzie."

Lizzie bobbed and left the room.

Felicia filled her cup and offered to do the same for Haley.

"I suppose I will," Haley said, handing her saucer over. "What I wouldn't give for a good strong cup of coffee right about now."

"You'll have to go to Italy for that, I hear," Felicia said. "Lizzie can make you the English version."

Haley wrinkled her nose. "Tea will suffice."

Felicia relaxed onto the settee, crossing one knee elegantly over the other. She addressed Ginger eagerly. "Wasn't last night just so exhilarating? My acting lessons had some worth after all."

Ginger couldn't hold in a grin at her sister-in-law's enthusiasm. "You and Haley both were exceptional."

"What did you find out at Scotland Yard?" Felicia continued.

Ginger shared a look of amusement with Haley. Such a dramatic change had come over Felicia, though Ginger wasn't sure how pleased she was that sleuthing had suddenly become Felicia's new source of distraction.

Ginger scrubbed Boss' neck as he lightly snored. "Superintendent Morris has made another arrest."

Felicia nearly jumped to her feet. "Cindy!"

Ginger eyed her with interest. "As a matter of fact, yes."

"I knew it," Felicia said. "She looks the envious type. Mrs. Reed had encroached on her territory."

"Well, I'm not sure about that," Ginger said carefully. "It has more to do with her pet snake."

Felicia's grin disappeared. "Oh?"

"Tell her, Haley," Ginger said.

"Emelia Reed's blood reports came in. There was an extraordinarily high level of protein in her blood."

"What does that mean?" Felicia asked.

"It's evidence pointing to the presence of snake venom."

Felicia fell back into the settee and covered her mouth with her palm. "Oh, my word!" She leaned toward Haley. "Mrs. Reed was bitten by Cindy's snake?"

"Perhaps," Ginger said. Something in the depth of her being felt like it would not be that simple.

Noise erupted in the entrance way and Ambrosia's voice echoed through the high ceilings. The click-tap of her walking stick on the marble floors grew louder, and a moment later, the family matron burst into the room.

Oh, mercy.

Gone was the Victorian bun piled high on Ambrosia's head and in its place a mar celled bob that tapered closely to the neck. A hairpin at the temple kept the short locks off her face.

Ambrosia's soft cheeks grew pink at her fashion revelation. "What do you think?"

The stunned pause continued.

"Grandmama!" Felicia finally managed. "You look fabulous."

Ginger agreed. "You do, it's just a dramatic change to take in."

Ambrosia's wrinkled lips pulled downward. "I'm a fool. The very picture of vanity! I can't believe I submitted myself to such frivolity. How can I possibly face anyone now? It'll take *years* to grow it back."

Ginger placed Boss on the floor and went to her grandmother-in-law. "Society will commend you, not condemn you. You're simply staying abreast of what's new this century. You must stand proud."

Ambrosia huffed. "I do hope you're right. Felicia, fetch Langley and have her bring tea to my room."

Ambrosia left, and there was a moment of silence before the sitting room erupted in a round of giggling.

GINGER WAS SURPRISED to meet Oliver coming down

the staircase as she made her way up to her room. "Oliver? When did you get here?" Boss, tucked under her arm, wiggled his little body toward the visitor.

"About an hour ago. Mr. Pippins let me in," he said as he stroked Boss, then addressed her questioning look. "I was just visiting Miss Hanson in the library."

"Oh, yes. So sad, isn't it. How is she today?"

"Quiet. The experience has been traumatic. All I could do was offer to pray."

"I'm sure you were a great comfort."

"I've invited her to visit me at St. George's anytime she likes. Perhaps, you could bring her along to a service with you."

"Of course. Once Miss Hanson is ready for excursions."

"She's worried about people discovering her secret, and I assured her that all the members of Hartigan House, including myself, will show the utmost discretion. She has God's forgiveness and can move forward in her life afresh."

"Agreed," Ginger said. "I promise to look after her. She's welcome to stay as long as she likes."

"Your kindness is commendable, Ginger."

Ginger patted his arm playfully. "Oh, stop that, Oliver."

"Where will I find your butler? I took a taxicab here. My old rattletrap is proving to be unreliable again."

Ginger wondered if she should take Oliver home. Then she could call in on Basil. Before Emelia's demise, Ginger and Basil would pop in to each other's houses uninvited all the time, "when they were in the area." She silently wondered if she'd still be welcomed. Basil's mood had changed so much, she'd begun doubting his intentions toward her. Had the last three happy months been a sham?

"Oh, I'm about to go out," Ginger said. "I can drive you."

Oliver replied to her offer. "I'd hate to inconvenience you."

"It's no inconvenience at all. Please wait for me in the sitting room, and I'll be down shortly."

Ginger placed Boss on the steps and he raced to the top, then sat on the landing to stare at her as she approached.

Taking a quick minute to look in on Matilda Hanson, Ginger turned toward the library. Miss Hanson sat in what had become her usual place in the chair by the window. Her legs were covered with a blanket, and she cradled a cup of tea. Oliver's discarded cup remained on the coffee table. Matilda looked thin and pale, but on the mend, thankfully. It had been a close call.

"Hello, Miss Hanson."

"I think you can call me Matilda by now," Matilda said with a slight smile. "You've seen me with my bloomers down."

Ginger chuckled. "You must be feeling better."

"I am. Stronger each day."

"I'm glad to hear it. How was your visit with the reverend?"

"Pleasant. He's a very nice man."

Felicia bounded inside and exclaimed, "There you all are! I was beginning to think I was alone in this big house." She plopped into an empty chair with a flourish, and Ginger envied her sister-in-law's energy. "Ginger, do tell me you have another exciting assignment for me. I get so frightfully bored."

"I'd rather hoped you had got this mode of excitement out of your system, Felicia," Ginger said. "It's really beneath your station, not to mention dangerous." Ginger held up a palm, "And please don't tell me I sound like Ambrosia."

"Well," Felicia pouted, "you do. I have no diversions, and I'm not going to marry any of the old oafs Grandmama has picked out for me."

"Then find your own old oaf," Ginger challenged. She couldn't help stepping into her big sister role. "Spend time where gentlemen do."

"Like church?"

"Why not?" Matilda Hanson said, surprising them both. "You're not likely to meet a philanderer there."

Ginger stared at the young woman. Was she, too, enamored with Oliver Hill?

"You can meet philanderers anywhere," Felicia said. "Even church."

"True," Ginger admitted. "But the ratio is bound to be far less."

OLIVER WAS WAITING PATIENTLY in the sitting room

when Ginger found him. "Sorry, for the delay. I ended up chatting with Miss Gold and Miss Hanson. I think Miss Hanson is doing better."

"Yes, and thank the Lord," Oliver said, standing.

"My Crossley's in the garage in the back." Ginger searched for Boss, who had returned on his own to the sitting room and was already curled up by the fireplace. "Oh Bossy, you lazy puppy! We're going for a motorcar ride."

Boss knew the word "motorcar" and was immediately up and following Ginger with canine anticipation. They found Pippins and Scout playing a pencil and paper game in the morning room.

"We're playing 'noughts and crosses' missus. Just for a few minutes over tea. It's all right, innit, missus?"

Ginger fondly remembered playing this same game with a much younger Pippins when she was a child. "So long as you've completed your schooling."

"The tutor phoned to say that he is ill, today, madam," Pippins explained.

"Very well. I'd hate to interfere with a good game of tic tac toe."

Oliver greeted the older man and young boy with questions about their well-being. "Each day I wake up is a good day, Reverend," Pippins said jovially.

Scout wasn't as perky about his future. "Is good here, Reverend 'ill. I miss my cousin."

"How about I come for a visit soon," Oliver said. "I hear there's a new horse on the premises."

"Oh, there is, Rev, and a real beauty, too!"

Ginger smiled at the exchange. "Whenever you're ready, *Rev*."

Ginger led Oliver down the cobbled path through the back garden to the garage where the Crossley was parked, noting how carefully Boss tried not to get underfoot. Ginger found the garage door unlocked and assumed Clement had been tending to the motorcar.

Suddenly, Boss began barking wildly.

"What is it, Boss?" Ginger turned to Oliver. "This is quite unlike him."

Boss was relentless, taking a stance near the back-seat on the driver's side and yipping madly. Ginger opened the door and screamed.

CHAPTER TWENTY-FIVE

a snake slithered out of the car, but Ginger slammed the door on it. The reptile's lifeless head dropped to the ground

"Good heavens!" Oliver said, holding a hand to his heart. "That did startle me."

Ginger had been more than a little startled too. She swept Boss off the ground and held him tightly. "How did a snake get into my motorcar?" She walked around the vehicle. All the doors were shut tight and the windows closed.

"Open the boot," Oliver said.

Ginger clicked it open. Empty. "It's sealed. Not a crack or crevice.

"Strange," Oliver said. "Do you think—?"

"Someone put it there."

Oliver grimaced. "But why on earth?"

"To send me a message," Ginger said grimly.

"A message about *what?*"

"I've been investigating the death of Emelia Reed. Basil asked me to help. She was poisoned with snake venom."

Oliver opened the door and looked closely at the grizzly remains—brown scales with black speckles, the length of the body remained on the seat while the head lay, mouth gaping, on the ground. "It's a common grass snake," Oliver said. "Harmless."

"Whoever did this meant to frighten me off," Ginger said. It also meant that her cover had been blown. It had to be someone from the club, but who? Conway? Nuala or Sorcha? Cindy was out of jail. Being a snake-lover, this might be an intimidation tactic. Where was she now, anyway? There'd been no sign of her at the club.

"I need to ring Basil," Ginger said. "I'm afraid you'll have to take a taxicab back to St. George's after all."

"Perhaps I'll stay until he arrives," Oliver said. Ginger noted the protective look in his eyes and the determination in his stance. "To protect the evidence, and all that."

Ginger wanted to hug her friend at that moment. "Thank you, Oliver."

GEORGE HARTIGAN'S STUDY, Ginger's study now, was a source of emotional comfort. Ginger's many childhood memories included spending time with her father in this room, him smoking a pipe as he wrote his business correspondence, and her curled up with a book in the cosy chair by the fireplace. If she closed her eyes and concentrated, she could see him sitting there dressed in a dark smoking jacket, his pipe hanging out of the corner of his mouth. She could even smell the tang of his tobacco.

She settled herself in her new office chair—Father's had been too big and worn out to use comfortably—and picked up the barbell-style receiver of her new telephone. She dialed Basil's home number, hoping he was there. He picked up after three rings.

"Reed."

"Hello, Basil. It's Ginger." Ginger relayed the disturbing discovery.

Basil's response was tense and abrupt. "I'll be right over."

Pippins was in the passageway, waiting, as he did, in case Ginger needed anything.

"Pips, did you notice anything unusual in the back garden this morning?" Ginger asked. "Perhaps someone you didn't recognize?"

"If I had, madam," the elderly man said, "I would've notified you immediately."

"Of course. Thank you."

"You might talk to Clement," Pippins said. "He's been working in the garden all morning. Perhaps he noticed something out of the ordinary. Would you like me to fetch him?"

"I can do it," Ginger said.

"Last I saw him, he was heading toward the rose garden."

CLEMENT WAS TENDING THE ROSES, wielding a pair of sharp secateurs and pruning the plants back mercilessly.

"Good day, Lady Gold." Clement straightened up stiffly when he spotted Ginger. In his fifties, he had strong arms and thinning hair. As far as Ginger knew, he'd never been married. "Is there something I can help you with?" he asked.

"Hello, Clement. Did you unlock the garage this morning, by any chance?"

"Indeed. I do every morning, madam, at six a.m. I make sure the Crossley is ready for you to drive should you wish." He wrinkled his nose in question. "Would you rather I didn't?"

"Normally, it's not a problem, but for the next while, you probably shouldn't."

Clement's brow furrowed further. "Did something happen?"

"Just a little prank. Did you happen to notice anyone in the back lane?"

"No, madam. It's been only young Scout and me out this way, caring for Goldmine."

Ginger found Scout in the stable, feeding Goldmine an apple from the palm of his hand. On seeing him, so small against the horse, her heart gave a maternal squeeze.

"Hello, Scout," she said.

"Oh, 'ello, missus. Me and Goldmine are just keeping each other company. I did my chores, you can ask Mr. Clement."

"And I'm sure you did a fine job," Ginger said with a smile. "While you were very busy working, did you happen to spy a stranger on the property? Perhaps around the garage?"

Scout's face crumpled in concentration, and he lapsed into his street parlance. "No, missus. I di'n't see nuffin' 'spicous."

"Well, if ever you do see someone you don't know on the property, let Mr. Clement know." She added protectively, "Don't approach them yourself."

Scout, always eager to please, nodded animatedly. "Yes, missus."

Ginger returned to Oliver who was dutifully keeping watch. "No one saw anyone or anything unusual this morning," she announced. "Clement unlocked the door at dawn."

BASIL ARRIVED with a dark mood of dismay. He looked surprised at seeing Oliver there, his gaze narrowing briefly.

Pippins hovered behind him, having let Basil into Hartigan House and leading him out to the back garden. Ginger nodded subtly, and the butler quietly made his leave.

"Oliver was here to pay a pastoral visit to Miss

Hanson," Ginger explained, "and I was about to drive him back to the church. We found this creature in the back seat of the Crossley."

Basil stared at the dismembered pieces. "What happened to it?"

Ginger explained the accidental decapitation.

Basil's hazel eyes tightened with concern. "You're in danger, Ginger."

"If I were truly in danger, this snake would've been venomous."

"Emelia died at the hands of whoever is responsible for this."

"That's an assumption," Ginger returned.

"An assumption with merit."

"I'm not stopping until this is solved."

"Ginger."

"Don't Ginger me. You've not been the same—"

Oliver cleared his throat. "I think I'll be heading off now."

Ginger grew crimson with embarrassment. She'd momentarily forgotten the vicar was still with them. Blast Basil! He was making her lose her senses!

"I'll see you out," Ginger said. She needed to get her wits about her.

By the time she'd returned, Basil had gathered the pieces of the snake and put them into an evidence bag. Even though he was working unofficially, certain things were habitual.

He sighed, and Ginger recognized his look. Resignation at not being able to control her. He hadn't been able to control Emelia, either. Basil appeared to attract women with strong personalities.

"I took the liberty of letting myself into Emelia's flat. I found this in her things."

He offered Ginger a booklet and she opened it. "Bank records?"

Basil nodded.

On further study, Ginger saw a pattern of deposits. She stared up at Basil. "Was she—?"

"I believe she may have been blackmailing people," Basil returned. "At least three if you can go by the regularity of the numbers."

"Is there any way of telling who the three people are?" Ginger asked.

Basil pointed to the booklet. "The entries have a notation."

"Yes, I see. Initials."

"I suspect that CS is Conway Sayer. JP, John Phillips; CW, Cynthia Webb. We need to find out what Emelia knew about them."

"Well, from what I could gather from the club's ledger," Ginger said, "Sayer is pilfering. If Charles Sabini ever got wind of that, Sayer would be as good as dead."

"Definitely motive."

"John Phillips is an American diplomat, but he doesn't seem terribly concerned about his reputation," Ginger mused. "Otherwise, he'd at least use an alias."

Basil agreed. "It must be something else then."

"I have no idea about Cynthia Webb," Ginger said. "What did the Yard find out about her?"

"That's the thing. They can't find anything on her at all. It seems her "real" name is just another alias."

"She's hiding something."

"She's not the only one, I suspect."

Pippins returned, caught Ginger's eye, and waited for her to acknowledge him.

"What is it Pips?"

"Miss Higgins on the line for you, madam. She says it's important."

She glanced at Basil. "If you'll excuse me."

Ginger hurried to her study to take the call. Haley never rang unless something pressing or pertinent came up.

"Hello, Haley," Ginger said.

"Ginger, good. You're there."

"What is it? Do you have news on Emelia Reed's case?"

"You might call it that. Jonathan Phillips is on my table. Dead. A snake bite on his neck."

CHAPTER TWENTY-SIX

There was nothing like death to suck the life out of one's personality. Once so pompous and charismatic, Jonathon Phillips' lifeless body lying flat and naked under a white sheet on the ceramic slab appeared smaller, his boisterous presence lost.

As usual, Haley didn't waste time on pleasantries and got right to the point.

"The bite mark on his neck matches the one found on Mrs. Reed precisely, leading me to believe it was from the same snake."

"Was Mr. Phillips restrained in any way?" Ginger asked.

Haley shook her head, and a strand of dark curls fell free from her casual faux bob. "There are no other suspicious lesions, however, unlike with Mrs. Reed, arsenic was found in his blood. Along with the extra protein that supports the venomous bite."

"He was poisoned first," Basil said. "Mr. Phillips was a strong man. Our killer incapacitated him before releasing the snake."

"It would appear that the killer was stronger than Emelia, able to restrain her with his or her own physical strength, but not stronger than Mr. Phillips," Haley said.

"Yes," Basil said. "But why not just kill him with arsenic? Why go to the trouble of the snake. It only ties him or her to Emelia's murder."

"It's personal," Ginger said. "Our killer isn't scared of having a secret revealed. He or she is angry on a deeper level."

Basil's studious hazel eyes landed on Ginger. "You could be right. The question is, how are John Phillips and my wife connected to this killer?"

"That is the question," Ginger said professionally, but inside she was stuck on the words, *my wife*. In the past three months, Basil had only referred to Emelia by her first name. He had never once called her his wife, at least not in Ginger's presence. She tucked her chin and averted her gaze.

Basil sighed before turning to Haley. "Any other points of interest to report?"

"Only that Scotland Yard will be here any moment."

"Oh, we'd better skedaddle," Ginger said. She gave Haley a quick hug. "Thanks for calling us first. You're a brick."

Haley cracked a smile. "I honestly don't see why the English think calling someone a brick is flattering."

Ginger managed a smile. "There is a lot that goes on around here I don't understand."

Basil slid her a sideways glance. Had he picked up on her double meaning?

Back in Basil's Austin, Ginger borrowed the rearview mirror. She straightened her hat, reinforced the curls of her bob against her cheek, and reapplied her lipstick. Then, feeling emboldened and confident she turned to Basil and asked, "What now?"

Basil directed his motorcar back toward Belgravia. "Let's visit the American Embassy and see what they have to say."

Ginger agreed this was a good next move.

The journey led them through Mayfair, past the Ritz Hotel along Green Park with the outline of Buckingham Palace in the distance. Ginger wondered what His Majesty was up to these days. She glimpsed a small crowd of well-dressed women on the pavement forming a half-circle around another lady wearing a white spring jacket and a red cloche hat. The group of women was obviously enraptured by whatever the woman in the red hat was saying.

"Pull over!" Ginger said.

"What?"

"Pull over. That woman in the red hat, is it Cynthia Webb?"

Basil leaned close to peer out of the passenger window, and Ginger couldn't ignore the warm, musky scent of his cologne.

Dang him!

"Her look is so altered, it's hard to tell at first, but I do believe you're right."

"Look at the billboard behind her. *Jeune et Belle*. That's the brand of face cream the girls use at the club."

Basil opened his door to step out, but Ginger stopped him. "She'll recognize you."

"What about you?"

"She only knows me as a blonde French woman."

Ginger hopped out of the Austin and blended in with the group of entranced ladies.

"Perhaps by looking at me, you would guess my age to be twenty-five, wouldn't you?" Cindy declared. "No. I'm nearly forty-five years old!

A gasp of surprise and a murmur of appreciation rose from the small crowd.

Ginger had seen Cindy's legs. There was no way she was forty-five.

"After a month of using *Jeune et Belle* face cream your wrinkles will smooth away, and your skin will tighten. Age spots and unsightly blemishes, gone! This formula is scientifically designed in the best beauty labs in Paris. Normally, a jar like this would sell for ten shillings! But today I'm offering you a special deal. One jar for five shillings. Or save even more when you buy more. Two for seven or three for ten! This opportunity will end when the supply does, so make sure to stock up today."

The women practically bowled one another over to purchase Cindy's beauty cream. Ginger shook her head.

LEE STRAUSS

Perplexed, Basil looked at Ginger as she closed the door behind her.

"My guess is that she's selling *udder salve* under the pretense of an expensive French beauty treatment."

"What makes you think that?" Basil asked.

"We saw John Phillips buy a large tin of it from Harrods. The color and texture of the jar of *Jeune et Belle* at the club is the same. She's added scent to make it seem like an expensive product from France."

Basil worked his lips. "Had John Phillips and Cynthia Webb been working on the swindle together?"

"Perhaps this confidence trickster no longer wanted to share the proceeds with her partner," Ginger said. "You wouldn't believe what's she's charging."

Basil concurred. "And maybe Emelia got in her way somehow."

"It could be what Emelia was blackmailing Cindy for."

"Fraud is a criminal offense," Basil said. "Cindy will be facing time in prison."

"Should we ring the police? She's fleecing all those women."

"We can call from the embassy, but I'm sure she'll be long gone by then."

As they entered Grosvener Gardens, Basil slowed his vehicle to negotiate around a lumbering horse and carriage. He stopped in front of number four, a lime and brick structure that housed the US embassy.

Under no illusion that they'd get past the reception,

or that they'd be given any information about the diplomat, Ginger knew that it never hurt to try.

Basil pulled out his police identification card. "I'm Chief Inspector Basil Reed. It's important that I see Ambassador Jonathon Phillips."

The receptionist, an intelligent-looking woman, had long hair pinned up into a faux bob and round, gold-rimmed glasses resting on full cheeks. She regarded Basil and Ginger carefully, her small eyes blinking slowly. "You mean Ambassador Henry Jenkins."

Basil glanced sideways at Ginger. Had they been duped?

"Mr. Jonathon Phillips is on staff at the embassy, but he's a secretary."

"I see," Basil said. "How long has Mr. Phillips been in the ambassador's employ?"

"Since January. Is there a problem? Should I pass a message along?"

"No, that's fine, madam. I'm sure you'll hear from Scotland Yard soon enough."

CHAPTER TWENTY-SEVEN

"So let me get this straight," Haley lounged on the sitting room settee; her flesh-colored stockings evident from the hem of her tweed skirt that landed below the knees. Her feet crossed at the ankles, and her arm draped languidly over the armrest. " John Phillips is not a diplomat. Cindy is selling udder salve as elite, age-defying face cream from Paris. John Phillips had an interest in Emelia. Cindy had an interest in Phillips."

"It would appear that Cindy is the killer." Ginger, like Haley, had her feet up on the ottoman, ankles crossed. In one hand she held a cut-crystal glass with one finger of bronze-colored brandy. The other hand rested on Boss' soft body as he snored blissfully on Ginger's lap.

"Will there be an arrest?"

"Basil is with Morris as we speak. But with Morris,

one never knows. I do plan to return to North Star for one more turn as Antoinette."

"What on earth for?"

Ginger scratched Boss under his collar and around his ears. She found it as calming as he did. "There's something that's bothering me about this case."

Haley's dark brow lifted. "You don't think Cindy is guilty?"

"Oh she's guilty, all right. I'm just not sure if it's of murder."

"A hunch?"

"For one thing, the murder weapon hasn't been found."

"Good point. According to evidence, Cindy's snake is indeed a wild scarlet and isn't venomous."

"Neither has the scene of the crime been determined, at least that we know of," Ginger said. "It's possible Morris has stumbled on it, but if he has, Basil's inside man hasn't mentioned it."

Haley sipped her brandy then said, "I guess I'm going to the club again. I've never seen so much burlesque in all my years."

"You and me both, Haley," Ginger lifted Boss and pressed her cheek against his head. "I'll be glad when this is done and over with."

HALEY HEADED upstairs in search of Felicia since both she and Ginger agreed that Felicia would be put out if not invited. Ginger's sister-in-law had proven to be an asset, and Ginger wanted to give her the opportunity to continue to prove herself. Hopefully, Felicia's wayward behavior was a thing of the past.

Ginger paused at the foot of the steps at the sight of a frazzled-looking Langley—Ambrosia's maid—scampering toward the drawing room with a plate of sandwiches in hand. Ambrosia's voice filtered through the door when the maid opened it, and if Ginger could go by Langley's demeanor, Ambrosia wasn't enjoying her visitor. Mrs. Schofield, Ginger suspected. She knocked before entering and had her suspicions verified.

"Hello, Mrs. Schofield." Ginger entered with Boss at her heels. "I thought it might be you enjoying tea with Grandmother."

Mrs. Schofield was a dainty white-haired lady with sharp eyes and bony fingers. Her hand trembled slightly as she lifted her teacup. "I heard that the Dowager Lady Gold had had her hair cut, so I just had to come over to see it for myself. Very *avant-garde*. On another lady of her generation, one would think it a poor attempt at holding on to one's youth, but we know your dear grandmother is anything but vain."

Ambrosia's face flushed several shades of red, and Ginger had to bite the inside of her cheek to keep from breaking out in laughter. Mrs. Schofield certainly had a way to conceal insults with flattery.

"Grandmother's new style is stunning, I agree," Ginger said. "I'm sure it will soon catch on for ladies of all ages wanting to stay fresh with the times."

Ambrosia gave Ginger a glance of appreciation and, dare Ginger say, gratitude.

Mrs. Schofield pursed her wrinkled lips and raised her teacup. "Perhaps you are correct. I might have to make an appointment with my hairstylist myself soon."

Ambrosia's round eyes sparkled with a look of triumph. "It would do wonders for you, Mrs. Schofield. Simply take *years* off." Ambrosia was on a roll. "My hairdresser also told me about a fabulous face cream from France, *Jeune et Belle*. It's quite difficult to come by, apparently. I purchased a year's supply."

Oh, mercy. Ginger covered her mouth to hold in the threatening chuckle. If Ambrosia ever discovered the cream she championed was cow udder salve, she'd simply die of humiliation.

CINDY WAS BACK at the club with Jake in tow. Ginger wondered why she chose to dance when it seemed like she was making loads of money with her face cream swindle. Ginger watched surreptitiously as the girls got ready. Conway stuck his head in without knocking. This wasn't unusual. What *was* unusual was the way he waved Cindy over and the heated discussion that followed.

"Jake is harmless. Ask one of the coppers."

Ginger couldn't hear Conway's response as they'd stepped further into the passageway. The way they spoke to each other was more familiar than was usual between an employer and employee. Perhaps there was a connection between the two that Ginger and Basil had missed.

Cindy insisted on closing the show and had a few unsavory words to say to one of the new dancers when she argued against the suggestion. Now that Cindy had been in held in custody for the suspicion of murder, the others gave her a wider berth.

Haley and Felicia were at their usual table minus Mr. Phillips, but plus Basil. Ginger sensed his protective nature toward them and smiled.

Nuala and Sorcha performed their bird and hunter routine, and a new girl did a Little Bo Peep number. Ginger's French maid song and dance had the crowd hooting and applauding until the curtain fell. Like the other dancers, she joined the crowd, nodding to her friends as she headed to the back by the bar. She wanted to get a wide-angle look at things.

Basil stood and retreated to the bar as well. The barman reappeared from the door behind the bar and was soon ready to serve them with the requisite folded white tea towel draped over his well-built shoulder. His blue eyes twinkled as he stared at Ginger. "What can I get you, *Antoinette*? It is Antoinette tonight?"

Ginger laughed a light sparkly laugh, keeping her French persona intact. "Of course it is, silly. Why would I be anyone else?"

When Billy attended to patrons at the other end of the bar, Ginger asked Basil, "Did your man find out anything about Billy Foster?"

Basil shook his head. "No one by the name of William or Billy Foster is known to the Met."

The piano player started Cindy's eastern-sounding dance tune, and the curtain rose to reveal Cindy in her colorful sari. The snake cage was covered and sat on a table to the side.

As Cindy dropped layers of her costume on the stage, Billy left to make their drinks. He returned shortly with a whisky for Basil and a cola for Ginger. Ginger's gaze locked onto the barman's crystal-blue eyes. They looked strangely familiar to her. "*Mon ami*," she said. "We were wrong about Cindy. She's not a murderess after all. So unkind of us to jump to conclusions."

Billy grunted. "Most interesting thing that has happened around here for a while."

"Did you know that Mr. Phillips is dead?" Basil asked.

Billy showed mild shock at the question. "The diplomat? Outraged husband finally caught up with him, eh?"

On stage, Cindy whipped off the cover of Jake's cage to the gasp of the crowd. She stealthily removed the reptile and wrapped it around her arms as her hips swiveled.

"He was bitten by a snake, the same as Destiny." Basil continued.

"Ain't that an odd coincidence," Billy said.

Then all hell broke loose.

CHAPTER TWENTY-EIGHT

Screams and shouts erupted. Tables were turned, drinks crashed to the floor. Women ran out of the doors.

Cindy lay crumpled on the stage.

"That's not part of her act," Ginger said. She and Basil dodged panicking customers and abandoned chairs.

A man shouted, "That snake bit her on the neck! It's on the loose."

Ginger and Basil ran to the stage.

The man was right. Two bite marks were evident on Cindy's ghostly white neck. Haley was already on stage checking for a pulse. She shook her head.

"She's gone."

"I thought wild scarlets were nonvenomous," Ginger said.

"They are," Haley said.

MURDER AT KENSINGTON GARDENS

Felicia disappeared backstage and returned with a waste bin in her hand.

"I've found Jake."

Ginger grimaced at the slithering reptile inside. "Someone swapped the wild scarlet for a coral snake. In this dim lighting, the slight difference in marking would be easy to miss."

"It's over here!" a man shouted.

"Stand back," Basil said. He dug out his identification card. "Scotland Yard."

"It's still moving!"

"Someone do something!"

A gunshot fired and the snake crumpled to the floor. The men in the room turned to the shooter. Ginger, as Antoinette, stood legs apart, arms firm and pistol smoking. "*Je suis désolée*, gentlemen. It's a gift from America." Ginger made a show of putting it back in her garter. "A girl must protect herself."

Basil's jaw dropped and closed again. "I never get used to you doing that."

"Nobody move!"

Ginger and Basil froze. Not because of the command but because of who the voice belonged to.

"We heard a revolver fire," Morris said.

Fingers pointed at Ginger.

Morris approached her, and though Ginger worked to keep him from gaining eye contact, she failed. Morris' heavy jaw dropped open in surprise as recognition dawned. "Well, well, well."

Morris had the upper hand. One word and he could

191

LEE STRAUSS

expose her and irreparably ruin her reputation. Desperate, she begged.

"Please, monsieur, I beg of you to keep a girl's secret."

"I told you to stay out of police business."

"I appeal to your sense of propriety."

Morris' jowls jiggled as he fought back a grin. He turned to his constable. "Arrest her."

"But, sir!" Basil protested. "She prevented a poisonous snake from taking another victim."

Morris was unmoved. "She killed the evidence."

"Sir!"

"Arrest him too!"

"On what charge?" Basil demanded.

"Obstructing a police investigation. I told you to stay out of it."

Ginger recognized the futility in resisting and held her hands in front of her. Good thing she had a good solicitor.

"Sorry, sir," Sergeant Scott muttered as he snapped the handcuffs on Basil.

As a constable marched Ginger and Basil out of the club, Felicia and Haley ran to Ginger's side.

"Are the cuffs really necessary?" Haley asked sternly.

"Just following orders, madam."

Ginger's gaze locked onto Haley's. "Call my solicitor."

"Oh, Ginger!" Felicia cried, following along. "This is ghastly! Grandmama will faint at the news."

"Don't tell her. Make an excuse for me," Ginger said over her shoulder. "A believable one!"

Out of the corner of her eye, Ginger saw Conway do something she'd never seen him do as he watched Morris lumber toward Cindy's body.

He smiled.

THE SMELL in the holding area of the police station hadn't improved since the last time she was there visiting Basil. Sweat, bad breath, and sickly sweet perfume came from her cellmate who was dressed in a skimpy dress, torn stockings and thick makeup around her eyes.

"Hi ya, sister," she'd said when Ginger was pushed into the cell with her. She was stretched out on the only bench, and didn't bother to make room. "Tough night on the streets, eh?"

Ginger's outfit garnered hoots and whistles from the male population as well.

Basil put a quick stop to that from his cell to the left of hers.

"Cut it out!"

"Or you'll what?"

Basil stripped out of his fine dinner jacket and rolled up his shirt sleeves revealing toned biceps. Perhaps he really had been a boxer at one time. The drunks had enough sense to back off. He shoved his jacket through the adjoining bars. "Put this on."

Ginger accepted Basil's offering and easily slipped

into it, wrapping the oversized coat around her body. It concealed her décolletage, however, it wasn't long enough to hide her legs.

"Constable," Basil called. "Get the lady a blanket."

Ginger's cellmate snorted. "Pfft, some lady." Her greasy hair rolled to the side, and she emitted a less than ladylike snore.

The blanket arrived. Ginger grimaced at the sharp odor then tied it around her waist. What she wouldn't give for a nice hot, bathtub soak, with pleasant smelling soaps.

Basil leaned against the bars.

"How long do you think Morris will keep us here?" Ginger asked.

"Who knows," Basil replied. "He's punishing us, me for sure, so it could be a while."

Ginger was glad she was given a telephone call and that her solicitor had answered at the late hour.

"At least he didn't give me away," Ginger said.

"Morris has a heart," Basil said, "even if it's a small one."

Ginger snuggled deeper into Basil's jacket, finding comfort in its warmth and the lingering scent of Basil's cologne. She took a deep breath then whispered, "Someone swapped Cindy's snake."

Basil nodded. "The question is who?"

"Conway Sayer was acting suspiciously tonight. More fidgety than usual. He showed no emotion over the death of one of his dancers or the upsetting of the club's evening."

"News like this can actually draw attention, bring in clients," Basil said.

"Exactly. I saw him *smile*. For the first time since I've met him."

Now that the drunks had joined Ginger's cellmate in a chorus of snores, Basil rolled down his sleeves, aggression no longer necessary. "We need to go back to Harrods Animal Kingdom," he said. "Maybe they've sold a coral snake recently and can give a description of the person who bought it."

Ginger tightened the smelly blanket to stave off the growing chill. "Surely, they're closed now."

"First thing in the morning," Basil said. "Assuming we've been let out by then."

Ginger didn't relish the idea of spending the night in custody, especially since her cellmate had no intention of sharing the bench.

"I've never been on this side of the bars before," she said.

Basil's hazel eyes raked her from head to toe. He scowled. "It's not a good look for you."

Ginger huffed. He didn't look that great either. Well, actually, he did, but drat the man.

The jangle of keys drew their attention.

"Lady Gold," the constable said as he worked the lock open. "You're free to go. Seems the superintendent agrees with the witnesses who say that shooting the poisonous snake was the sensible thing to do. There's a taxicab waiting."

"Oh, thank goodness!"

Ginger turned to her cellmate and carefully laid the blanket over the woman's thin form. Her eyes cracked open. "See ya later, sister."

"What about me?" Basil said when the constable failed to open his cell.

"Sorry, Chief Inspector. Superintendent Morris said to leave you in. Apparently, you need to learn a lesson."

Basil growled and hit the bars with the soft side of his fist.

"I'll fetch you in the morning," Ginger said. She added a silent prayer of thanks for her miracle-working solicitor.

CHAPTER TWENTY-NINE

*H*aving indulged in the hot bath the night before and a short brandy with Haley to rehash the night's events, Ginger slept like a baby. She awoke to Boss licking her ear as if he were reminding her that she had an important errand to run.

She sat up straight. Harrods Animal Kingdom.

Boss sat upright, his stub of a tail wagging, big brown eyes hopeful.

"Oh, Bossy, I'm sorry. You can't come with me this time. I wouldn't want you to get eaten by a crocodile or stomped on by an elephant."

Boss had the good sense to whimper as he flattened himself on the bed. Ginger scrubbed his ears and kissed the top of his soft black head.

"Next time I go somewhere, I promise to take you."

Ginger dressed quickly and headed straight to her

study where she rang Basil. Six rings and no answer. *Drat! Where are you, Basil?* Had he gone to Harrods without her? Or perhaps Morris hadn't yet released Basil from custody. She rang the police station.

"Hello. This is Lady Gold. Has Chief Inspector Basil Reed been released?"

"Er, no, madam. The superintendent wants to hold him until dusk."

"Whatever for! He's committed no crime!"

"The superintendent begs to differ. If it's any consolation madam, the chief inspector's solicitor has been to visit."

"Thank you. Please let him know I've called, and that I'm heading to Harrods."

"Yes, madam."

Mrs. Beasley had tea and crumpets waiting in the morning room. "I heard you were up early today, m'lady. I can whip up eggs and bacon in a jiffy."

"Not for me. I'll eat a late breakfast when I return." Ginger sipped the tea and picked up a crumpet, which she ate while heading out to her Crossley. Clement was there, looking under the bonnet.

"Good morning, Clement. Is everything all right with the motorcar?"

"I was just checking it for you, madam."

"No unaccounted-for reptiles I hope?"

"No, madam, but the door lock had been jimmied open. Someone's siphoned off the petrol."

Ginger stomped her foot. Someone really wanted to

keep her from investigating further, which only made her more determined.

"I'll take a taxicab."

FORTUNATELY, Harrods wasn't that far away from Hartigan House. Though the store was massive, Ginger now knew her way and navigated quickly to the fourth floor to the motley mammalian and reptilian crew.

Ginger kept a look out for Basil in case, if by some miracle, he had been released from custody and made his way directly to the Animal Kingdom. She didn't find him, but she did manage to track down the salesman they had spoken to before.

"Mr. Long!"

Mr. Long's eyes flashed with annoyance for just a fraction of a second before taking on an exaggerated look of welcome.

"Hello again, Lady Gold. What can I help you with this time?"

"I'm looking for someone who bought a coral snake, perhaps recently."

Mr. Long's lips pulled down as he shook his head. "Sorry, madam."

"Are you certain? I don't know if you've heard about the incident that happened yesterday, but a woman was killed."

Mr. Long's lips twitched, and Ginger felt certain he was about to lie to her again.

"You won't get into trouble with me, Mr. Long. I'm only a private investigator. I promise to keep your confidences."

With a sideways nod of his head, Mr. Long led Ginger to a quieter spot in the store. "Between you, me and the gate post, there was a man in a couple of days ago. Sometimes I make a deal on the side see, charge a little extra and keep a little for myself." A film of sweat formed on the man's upper lip. "The boss doesn't know, and I'd get fired if word got out. That's why I lied to the big man from Scotland Yard."

"Superintendent Morris was here?"

"First thing this morning while the doors were being unlocked."

Ginger's garage intruder may have done her a favor after all. Running into Morris this morning would've been disastrous.

"Did you get the man's name?"

Mr. Long shook his head. "He said he'd pay cash if I didn't ask questions."

"What did this guy look like?"

A shrug. "He wore a trench coat and a trilby, pulled low, like. Average height and weight."

"Eye color?"

The man wrinkled his nose. "I don't look into a man's eyes, madam."

Ginger sighed. Mr. Long wasn't giving her a lot to go on.

"He actually bought two. I had no idea what he

meant to do with them. I really thought he wanted them as pets."

Mr. Long removed a handkerchief from his suit pocket and mopped his face. "If it's any consolation, I'm truly sorry to hear about the girl's death, even if she was a loose woman."

inger felt herself to be somewhat brazen, walking into the North Star club through the employee entrance as Lady Gold—Antoinette and Georgia were no longer necessary. Whoever put the snake in her motorcar yesterday and stole her petrol that morning knew who she was anyway. In a moment of spontaneity, she'd got the taxicab driver to drop her off here instead of taking her home.

The light from outside was blinding, and when the door shut, she was left in complete darkness. As she waited for her eyes to adjust, she reached out her fingers along the wall where she swore she'd spotted an electric light switch. Fumbling, her fingers ran along chipped paint and cobwebs before locating what they were looking for. To Ginger's relief, the light clicked on, though it crackled and pulsed as if the filament was about to burn out any minute.

The club appeared empty, confusing since the back door was unlocked. A cleaner had been through as the chairs were all placed upside down on the tables, and the carpets had been vacuumed. The passageway to the backstage area and the offices was eerily quiet. Morris had absconded with her Remington pistol, so she dug out the German Böker trench knife she'd acquired during the Great War. The carbon-steel blade was secure in its sheath and tucked within easy reach in her handbag, Ginger decided to make her presence known.

"Mr. Sayer?"

A light flicked on in Conway Sayer's office.

"Mr. Sayer? Are you there?"

Conway Sayer stumbled out of his office, hair tousled, eyes cracking open painfully at the bright light. "What the dickens? Who's that?"

"Mr. Sayer, are you all right?"

"Just catching a bit of shuteye. Late nights at the club." He spat on his palm and mopped his hair back. "How did you get in here?"

"The back door wasn't locked."

"Blast. I must've forgotten to lock it."

Ginger narrowed her eyes. "You? That seems very unlike you." Ginger suspected someone else with a key had also paid a visit while the manager slept. *One of Sabini's men perhaps? Were they catching on to Sayer's thievery? If so, Conway Sayer was quite lucky to still be alive.*

"How would you know what I'm like?" Sayer demanded. "Who are you?"

"I'm Lady Gold, also known as—" she switched her accent to French, "Antoinette," and, pulling out her American twang, "Georgia."

Sayer's blood-shot eyes shut and snapped open again. "*What?*"

"I'm a private detective working on the Emelia Reed case. The victim was known here as "Destiny.'"

Sayer grew stone-faced. "I had nothing to do with that."

"This club is owned by Charles Sabini, is it not?"

With a lazy shrug, Conway said, "What of it?"

"He's the head of the Italian mafia here in London," Ginger said. "Guilty of many crimes, but has yet to be convicted of any of them. If he wants someone gone, they have a way of mysteriously disappearing."

Sayer's shoulders tightened, and his neck seemed to disappear. He glared at her. "I don't know what you're getting at, Lady Gold, but you're trespassing. You'd best be leaving, or I'll be forced to call the coppers."

Ginger ignored the threat. "It's come to my attention, Mr. Sayer, that you've been cooking the books."

Even in the dim lighting, Ginger could see Conway blanch several shades whiter.

"And I think Emelia Reed, alias Destiny, found out about it and blackmailed you for her silence."

"Steady on. I didn't kill her."

"Cindy found out too. Or perhaps she helped you kill Emelia but wanted something more. A cut of your illicit earnings.

"No," Conway's tired eyes flashed with fear. "I didn't

kill anyone."

"You bought a couple of poisonous coral snakes, didn't you? You used one to kill Emelia Reed, and the other to kill Cindy."

"No! You've got it all wrong! Yes, I'm pilfering, petty theft really, but I'm not a murderer! Besides, I can't stand snakes."

Ginger arched a brow.

"Look, I don't know what your game is, madam. Do you intend to blackmail me as well?"

"So you admit to being blackmailed."

"Drat! Yes, okay. Destiny was a Nosy Parker, and she had me cornered, but I was paying her."

"That's means, opportunity, and motive, Mr. Sayer. A jury just might hang you."

"How do you know it wasn't Cindy herself? It was *her* snake. And she hated Destiny. I wasn't the only one the witch was squeezing."

"What did Destiny have on Cindy?"

"She was in the country illegally. Broke some law in Virginia and didn't want to do time. Somehow she got smuggled into England. Destiny was going to get her deported."

This was interesting news. Had Mr. Phillips, the fake American diplomat, assisted Cindy's passage from America? Phillips bought udder salve, and Cindy sold it as face cream. Perhaps she had double-crossed him. She had treated the man with a certain amount of animosity that last time Ginger had seen them in the club together.

Cindy's accent had been clearly north London, but she could have been putting it on, just like Ginger had with her aliases. Had Superintendent Morris blundered by releasing her too soon? Phillips might've had motive to kill Cindy, but he'd already been dead for several hours before Cindy's demise.

Conway Sayer rubbed the back of his neck. "Come to think of it, and this may be nothin', but Billy asked me if Cindy had an extra cage lying around."

"Did she?"

"No. I told Billy to ask Cindy himself."

"And you never thought to ask what he wanted it for?"

"None of my business."

"Do you know where Billy lives?" Ginger asked.

"Same place as the girls. The Johnson Building."

Ginger shook her head. "If he's there, he's not receiving post." She remembered the names Basil had read out. Then her heart stuttered to a stop. The pieces suddenly fell into place. She and Basil had been looking at this case the wrong way all along.

"He's due into work any minute," Conway said. "You can ask him yourself."

"That's fine Mr. Sayer. Please don't mention to him that you saw me here."

The Johnson Building was around the corner from the club, making it easier to walk to than dealing with the traffic. Ginger strode toward it as fast as her Italian shoes could take her.

CHAPTER THIRTY-ONE

*G*inger waited across the street and out of sight until Billy Foster left the Johnson Building and walked away in the direction of the club.

As luck would have it, the caretaker was walking through the lobby of the building just as Ginger got to the entrance. She pounded on the door, the heat of her breath shooting quick spots of condensation on the glass.

Frowning, the caretaker opened the door to her.

"Hello, sir. Do you remember me? I was here a couple of days ago to visit friends and silly me, I left my handbag behind."

The caretaker's gaze dropped to the handbag over Ginger's shoulder. "Not this one. Another one."

He waved her in and then continued on his way down the hall, whistling "Near the South Sea Moon."

Ginger studied the names on the letterboxes and

found the one she was looking for. W. Phillips, 304. Though she'd barely caught her breath from her jaunt over from the club, she hurried up the stairs.

Those ocean-blue eyes. She should've put it together earlier. Billy Foster had the same blue eyes as John Phillips. Had she seen them standing side by side, the resemblance would've been obvious.

The question was, why had Billy killed his father?

Ginger trod quietly up the stairs making it to the second floor just as female voices filled the passageway. Ginger recognized the Irish lilt of Nuala's voice and Sorcha's laugh.

Of all the bad luck. Ginger would have to run into the two ladies in the building that she knew.

But they didn't know her. Not as Ginger. Ginger stood tall and walked confidently as if she had every reason in the world to be there. Sorcha and Nuala gave her a questioning glance but continued down the stairs without breaking stride or looking back.

The third floor was quiet. Ginger waited for sounds and noises that indicated other flats besides Billy Foster's were occupied or worse, had occupants readying to leave, but all was quiet.

She carefully picked the lock with her trusty hatpins and slipped inside.

Billy's flat smelled stale and stuffy, of masculine sweat, aftershave, and burnt toast. His level of tidying landed between the cosmic mess of Nuala and Sorcha and the ultra-tidiness of Cynthia Webb. A bedsit, it didn't have a bedroom, just a sofa bed folded up, and the bedding piled neatly at one end.

If Billy Foster had used a poisonous snake as a murder weapon, surely there would be evidence of it in the flat. If Billy had purchased two snakes, one of them might still be around, but there were no reptile cages or terrariums.

The kitchen consisted only of a small countertop, a toaster, a two-burner hot plate and a small pantry. She opened the pantry and jerked to the side. Staring back at her was the head of a coral snake, yellow slit eyes staring morbidly.

"Now this is a surprise."

Ginger slammed the pantry door shut and spun toward Billy's voice. He'd removed his shoes, which had muted his footsteps. The door to the bedsit was closed and Ginger wondered how far her screams would reach beyond it. Her heart thudded as the seriousness of her situation gripped her.

Billy stepped closer, and Ginger stepped back. Pressed against the window, she reached into her handbag and fingered the button to release the strap that secured the knife to the sheath.

Billy lifted a palm in peace. "I'm just getting something to drink. Would you like a whisky?"

"No thank you."

Billy removed a glass bottle from the pantry, twisted off the cap and poured the last of the amber liquid into a glass.

"Was Emelia Reed blackmailing you?"

Billy downed the whisky and wiped his mouth with the back of his hand. "Who? Oh, that doxy, Destiny. No."

"Why did you kill her then?"

"Because she was a stupid woman, that's why. Led me on, made me believe she cared for me and said she'd leave her stupid husband for me. She told me he was a boring accountant. How was I to know he was a copper? And *then* she took up with my useless old man!" His face bloomed red with his apparent humiliation.

"Did you kill her here?"

Billy took another step toward her, and Ginger sidestepped toward the door. He nodded in response to her question. "It's where I keep my snake head."

"And your father?"

Billy's head snapped up. "You're pretty bright, *Georgia*. No, wait. They call you Lady Gold, don't they? *Ginger?*

A shiver shot down Ginger's spine. Billy had been looking into her. *Of course*, he knew who she was. *He knew where she lived.* Bile shot up the back of her throat.

"John Phillips was my father in name only. Left me and my ma when I was a baby, went back to America where the money was. Never sent back a damn cent to support his illegitimate son. My mother pretended to have married him, took the name Mrs. Phillips just so she'd be treated kindly. It's better to be a widow than a ruined woman, you know? We meant nothing to him. When he came into the North Star a couple of months ago, with all his airs, I knew exactly who he was. I see him every day when I look in the mirror."

It was true, Billy had his father's ocean-blue eyes. John Phillips had been too blind or too conceited to even consider his son might be in London, much less the same club.

"I knew he'd be harder to subdue, so I added a little something to his drink first."

That explained the arsenic found in John Phillips' system.

Billy huffed. "The fool thought I'd invited him here to play family."

"What did Cindy have to do with anything?"

"John Phillips 'smuggled' Cindy into England," Billy said. "She was just another stupid doxy fling like my mother. They had this face cream swindle going, you know? Sold the stuff farmers smear on cow teats. I worked on a farm as a kid, so I knew what it was. When I caught her adding perfume to a tin of bag balm, I laughed out loud. Cindy swore me to secrecy, but when I wanted a cut for my silence, she and John Phillips refused.

He grinned crookedly. "I'm going to take over the family business now, you could say."

Billy Foster was telling her too much. It was clear he didn't plan on keeping her alive.

"Why snake venom?" she asked. She needed to keep him talking, but she also wanted to know.

"Creative, eh? My father thought he was *so* classy. I thought I'd bring him and his women down a peg."

Billy opened the pantry, but instead of getting another bottle of spirits, he removed the plate with the snake's head.

"Did you know that venom remains in the jaws of a snake after it's dead?"

He placed the plate on the counter and removed a pair of leather gloves from his jacket pocket. "Extra tough leather," he explained. "For my own protection, you see." He smiled at her as if they were best friends having a nice visit. He opened a wobbly kitchen drawer and removed a ball of twine. "It's best for you if you don't fight back."

Even with one bad leg, Billy had a long, strong stride. Ginger darted around the small table, whipped out her knife and tossed the steel-tipped leather sheath onto the floor. She gripped the knife tightly in her right hand, the blade sticking out from the soft side of her fist.

"Stay back."

"Whoa." Billy stilled. "Aren't you just one surprise after another?"

"I am, Mr. Foster. I'll warn you. I'm no stranger with a knife."

"So you've carved a goose?" Billy laughed. "You've definitely got pluck, I'll give you that." He stepped to the right, she mirrored his movement in the opposite direction.

"I'm warning you, Mr. Foster. I once stabbed a German intruder in France, straight through the heart."

Billy studied the weapon with interest. "Is that a

Böker? How on earth did you get a German trench knife?"

"You don't want to know."

With the strength of one arm, he upended the table. It hit the floor with a crash, and Ginger just barely managed to jump out of the way of it landing on her foot. She ran for the door. It was locked. She struggled with the handle, but the time spent allowed Billy to catch her.

He pushed her against the wall, and his lips pulled into a smarmy smile as he held her captive, his fists tight around her wrists.

His breath was hot and stunk of booze. "Drop the knife, Lady Gold."

CHAPTER THIRTY-TWO

*B*illy's blue eyes grew icy cold. "I said drop it."

"If you say so," Ginger said. She stretched out her fingers letting the knife go, point downward.

Releasing her, Billy let out a blood-curdling yell. The blade of her knife stood upright from his good foot. He swooped down to remove the weapon, and in doing so, revealed the nape of his neck. Ginger struck the spot with the edge of her hand, and Billy crumpled to the floor.

The door swung open and a startled and bewildered Basil Reed stared inside. "Oh, my God, Ginger!" Basil's voice echoed through the small room.

A wave of relief washed over Ginger. Basil had found her, but how did he know she'd be here?

"Basil, how—"

"As soon as Morris let me out I rang Hartigan

House. Pippins said you took a taxicab to Harrods. I immediately went there, and when I didn't find you, I threatened Mr. Long with his life to tell me what he knew. I wagered a guess you'd go back to the club, and Sayer told me you came here. You could've been killed!"

Ginger glanced at the unconscious form on the floor. "I know how to take care of myself."

Basil ran a hand through his hair, knocking off his hat. "How? *How* do you know?"

Ginger stared back but said nothing. The British secret service was extremely particular on the *secret* part of its name.

Scanning the floor for her discarded sheath, she spotted it under one of the wooden kitchen chairs, picked it up, and slipped her trench knife inside before returning it to her handbag. She smoothed out her jade-green rayon skirt, adjusted her hat, removed a tube of lipstick from her handbag, and reapplied the frosted pink.

Basil swooped up the ball of twine that had fallen to the floor and made a good show of tying Billy Foster's wrists tightly together. With a distinctly irritated voice he asked, "Well, are you going to at least tell me why Foster's on the floor?"

Ginger pointed to the snake head on the counter. "Murder weapon number one. Did you know that venom remains in the jaws even after the snake is dead? After Mr. Foster restrained his victims, he pressed the open jaw of the dead reptile against their neck. With Cynthia Webb, of course, the snake was alive."

Basil paced like a caged animal. "You could've been killed."

"You mean, I could've killed *him*." As if on cue, Billy Foster emitted a soft groan.

"Ginger Gold, you are exasperating!"

Ignoring Basil's outburst, Ginger said calmly, "Perhaps we should call for an ambulance. Or the police."

Basil glared. Under normal circumstances, he *was* the police.

"I'm going to look for a police box." Basil handed her his pistol. "Just in case."

She aimed it at Billy Foster.

CHAPTER THIRTY-THREE

Superintendent Morris had arrested Mr. Foster for the murder of Emelia Reed, Jonathon Phillips, and Cynthia Webb, known in Virgina as Cindy Webster. His displeasure—and humiliation that Ginger had solved the murder—was apparent in the purple shade of his skin. He pointed a chubby finger in her direction.

"Lady Gold, had this turned out differently, I wouldn't hesitate to throw your pretty interfering head in jail! Again!"

She offered an ingratiating smile. "You're quite welcome, Superintendent."

Ginger had made one last trip to the North Star to return the ledger to Conway Sayer. She admonished him to quit such practices of pilfering from dangerous mafia-type men if he valued his life. Hopefully, he would heed her words of warning.

Ginger's mind had been so busy she didn't even notice that Goldmine had brought her through their regular riding pattern through Hyde Park and back to the Hartigan House stables. Scout waited for her.

The lad had changed since coming to live with Ginger. He'd put on weight and even grown an inch or two. His speech was more precise and he dropped his 'h's' far less often.

However, he was far less eager, and his smile more hard-earned. Perhaps this was because he no longer had to please people to fill his stomach. Perhaps, despite the improvement of his surroundings, the safety and security Ginger provided, he was just sad.

"Hello, Scout."

Scout's eyes brightened when he saw Ginger and Goldmine approach.

"I can cool down the ol' boy for you, missus."

"That would be terrific." Ginger handed over the reins. "Maybe later, another lesson for you."

"If you don't mind, missus. I think I'm getting the 'ang—*hang*—of it."

Ginger found Clement in the hothouse she had recently had built at the gardener's request. "Scout's with Goldmine," she said. "Please go and check up on him in a few minutes."

Clement bowed his head. "Yes, madam."

Ginger found Haley, Felicia, and Ambrosia having a late breakfast in the morning room.

"How was your ride?" Haley asked.

"Splendid."

Lizzie appeared with a new pot of tea for Ginger with Mrs. Beasley right behind her.

"I saw you through the window, madam, and fried up some more eggs and kippers for you."

"Thank you, Mrs. Beasley," Ginger said.

Haley snapped the newspaper she'd been gripping. "The Paris Olympics are going well for Great Britain," she said. "Not as well as the United States, mind you."

"Lady Gold?"

Ginger turned at the sound of Matilda Hanson's voice.

"Miss Hanson, please join us."

Miss Hanson stood before them dressed in a coat and hat, gloves on, ready to go somewhere. "I have a taxicab waiting," she said. "I'm leaving Hartigan House, and I just wanted to say thank you, to you all, for everything."

Ginger rose from the table. "*You're leaving*? Where are you going?"

"I have a sister in Whitechapel. I'm going to work in her husband's butcher's shop until the next term starts. She doesn't know . . . No one knows . . . I can start over."

Ginger, Haley, and Felicia went to Matilda and gave her a warm hug.

"All the best to you," Haley said.

"Thank you, Miss Higgins. I won't forget that you saved my life."

Ginger linked her arm through Matilda's. "I'll walk you to the door."

Ambrosia remained seated but did say a friendly farewell, though Ginger could sense the matron's relief.

The taxicab had no sooner left when another pulled up in front of the gate.

Ginger couldn't believe her eyes. "Louisa?"

Before her, beaming, with green eyes like Ginger's own, stood a younger, brunette version of herself. Louisa's face had matured in the ten months since Ginger had last seen her.

"What are you doing here?"

"Ginger! I wrote to you that I would visit."

"But I thought you meant to finish your education first?"

"I detest university. *Life* is my education. Ginger, did you even miss me?"

Ginger embraced her half-sister. "Of course. I'm just surprised."

"Good!" Louisa spoke loudly in Ginger's ear. "Then I accomplished my goal. I wanted to surprise you."

"Does Sally know you've come?" Ginger couldn't imagine her stepmother being all right with this. At least Louisa had brought her maid, Jenny, who stood behind her with head bowed and hands full with a jewelry box and a hatbox.

"She does now. I sent her a telegram from the SS *Rosa*. That's the steamship you came over on, isn't it? Jenny and I spent the night in Liverpool. Horrible place, by the way. London is much more exciting. Are you going to invite me in?"

"Yes, of course, come in."

Louisa took in the grand entrance with obvious admiration. "Daddy sure took care of you."

"This is my childhood home," Ginger said, somewhat defensively. It wasn't like their father hadn't left Louisa an inheritance. She shared their Boston brownstone with her mother."

The commotion drew the attention of Pippins and the ladies in the morning room, and Ambrosia, Felicia and Haley filed in.

"I thought Miss Hanson was leaving," Ambrosia said.

"She did. This is Louisa, my American sister."

Ambrosia muttered, "It's like Piccadilly Circus around here."

"Look, Haley," Ginger said, waving Haley closer. "It's my sister Louisa. Louisa, you remember Miss Higgins."

"Of course I do!" Louisa gushed. " Darling, Haley! So good to see you again!"

The two of them embraced, and Haley caught Ginger's look over Louisa's shoulder. Oh, mercy!

"This is my sister-in-law, Felicia," Ginger said once Louisa had released Haley, "and my Grandmother, Lady Gold."

"Two Lady Golds," Louisa said. "That must get confusing, or do you still go by Mrs. Gold? I wouldn't if I were you. I've heard pompous titles go a long way here in the old country."

Ambrosia bristled and spoke under her breath to Felicia. "Americans have no manners."

"Oh, Grandmama," Felicia said, not bothering to lower her voice. "Miss Higgins is American and very polite."

"Perhaps we can all have tea in the drawing room," Ginger said. "Pippins, please ask Clement to help bring in Miss Hartigan's things. Grace, please clean Miss Hanson's old room and let me know when it's ready."

"Ginger, darling," Louisa said with a squeal. "You must give me a tour before tea. And I'll have coffee if they serve it around here."

Ginger shared an exasperated look with Haley, and Haley just grinned. "I'll wait with Felicia and Lady Gold in the drawing room."

There was another knock on the door, and Ginger was beginning to agree with Ambrosia's assessment of the frequent activity currently transpiring at Hartigan House. Louisa looked at her impatiently. "Don't you have a butler for that?"

"He's busy carrying your bags upstairs." Ginger opened the door to Oliver Hill.

"Oliver?"

"Oh, you've forgotten," he said graciously. "I'm here to see young Mr. Elliot."

"Oh yes, do come in." Ginger said. "It's been busy around here today. Miss Hanson has left—"

"Yes, she mentioned her intentions to me when I was here last," Oliver said.

"And my sister has arrived quite unexpectedly. Miss Hartigan, Reverend Hill."

Oliver extended his hand to Louisa. "It's a pleasure."

"My, Ginger, you never mentioned in your letters how handsome your vicar was. I might've come to London sooner."

Oliver's fair skin blossomed a deeper shade of pink. Ginger held in a chuckle. British ladies were far more conservative.

Oliver's gaze lingered on Louisa. "Are you staying in London long?" he asked.

Louisa giggled. "As long as Ginger can bear to have me around."

"I hope it's a long time then."

Ginger cleared her throat. "You'll find Scout in the garden, Oliver. Quite likely he's still in the stable."

"Nice to meet you Reverend Hill," Louisa said. Her voice echoed across the high ceilings as Ginger grasped her sister's arm and led her toward the drawing room. "Oh, please tell me he's not married."

Ginger groaned. There was no way Oliver hadn't heard that.

"Daddy never brought me to London before," Louisa lamented once tea had been served. "He said the ride over was terrible for Ginger when she was little and wouldn't put me through the trauma. Daddy was so kind. But London *is* rather fabulous, I'm a little put out now that I missed being here. Everyone speaks with such an adorable accent!"

"Do take a breath to eat a sandwich, love," Ginger said.

"Like you Ginger," Louisa continued, ignoring

Ginger's attempt to calm her. "Your American accent is all but gone. I wonder if I'll lose mine over time."

Ambrosia looked alarmed. "How long do you plan on staying?"

"For the summer at least. I told Mama I've had it with her rules. I've got my own money and I don't need her to boss me around. Speaking of Boss, where is the little dog? He's not—" Louisa grimaced as she imagined the worst.

"Boss is in the garden," Ginger said. "He quite loves it here."

"I'm relieved." She turned to Felicia. "You must just love living in London. And such a lovely day. I heard it did nothing but rain here."

Felicia, used to being the most vivacious presence in the room, stared at Louisa with a baffled expression. "London is fabulous, but I hear Boston is wonderful."

"Oh, it is. But the people there don't sit around and drink tea all day."

Ambrosia smoothed out the taffeta skirt of her day dress with stiff strokes and shot Louisa a haughty look of disdain. "We don't drink tea *all* day."

CHAPTER THIRTY-FOUR

*L*ouisa Hartigan had taken to life in London like milk and sugar to tea. Felicia had shown her the shopping district and the nightlife—however, she promised Ginger they wouldn't go near the seedier clubs where women took off their clothes. Only the places were modern girls liked to spend their time and have fun. Louisa even went to church with Ginger though Ginger suspected that had more to do with the vicar than God.

All in all, Louisa's presence was less upsetting than Ginger had expected. Sally was even mollified after several telegrams.

"I could see myself becoming a full-time Londoner," Louisa announced as they shared coffee together in the sitting room.

Ginger stroked Boss who was curled up on her lap. "You would miss Boston and your mother over time."

Louisa huffed. "I don't miss them at all."

"You've only been here two weeks."

"I think you underestimate my ability to know my own mind, Ginger. Oliver says he admires a woman who knows her own mind."

"*Oliver?*" Ginger said, hearing the shock in her voice. "You're on first name terms already?"

Louisa's eyes glinted mischievously. "I'd make a dramatic vicar's wife don't you think? The vicarage is really rather quaint."

Ginger shuddered with alarm. "You've been inside his vicarage?"

Louisa laughed. "You should see your face! I've only just peeked in the windows."

Ginger shook her head, then sipped her coffee. Louisa's time at Hartigan House would either keep Ginger young or give her grey hair.

Pippins quietly interrupted. "The chief inspector is here to see you, madam."

Ginger's heart leapt into her throat. The funeral was over.

It was over.

Ginger had been torn about whether she should go to Emelia Reed's funeral or not, but in the end, she'd decided that she'd honor Emelia's memory more by not attending. It turned out that Basil agreed. He'd placated Ginger by saying that everyone at the funeral represented his past. Ginger represented his future.

"Excuse me, Louisa," Ginger said.

Basil waited in the entrance hall, trilby in hand. He wore a handsome, tailored suit, cuffed trouser legs just touching his black leather shoes.

"Basil?"

"Hello, Ginger."

"We can sit in the drawing room," Ginger said, as the sitting room was occupied.

"Actually, I can't stay long."

"Oh." Ginger didn't want to speak in the echoing entrance hall. "Let's go outside then." She gathered her spring jacket and closed the front door behind them. Basil faced her as they stood on the front step.

"How was it?" Ginger asked, referring to the funeral.

"Good. Sad. Very sad. But, it was nicely done. Small. Just family."

Ginger didn't know what to say to that, so merely nodded.

"Morris doesn't want me coming back to work yet," Basil said. "He's still put out that I worked on the case when he had forbidden me to."

"More like he's put out with me and taking it out on you."

"Perhaps." Basil sighed and stared hard at Ginger. "I'm going away for a while."

"Alone?" Ginger said to her surprise. What she really meant was, *without me?*

"I need some time."

"Of course," Ginger said, working hard to keep her composure. "There's your season of mourning to think about. It would be unbecoming for a chief inspector to be seen out with another woman when the body of his dead wife is barely cold. I mean, what would people think?"

"I don't care what people think, Ginger. I just need some time."

"So you've said."

"I'm not sure how long I'll be away."

The earth stopped spinning. "What do you mean? Where are you going, exactly?"

"South Africa."

"*South Africa?* You plan to be away a while, then?" One didn't go to South Africa for a quick time of respite.

"I don't expect you to wait for me."

Ginger felt as if Basil had just slapped her with his glove.

"All I've been doing is waiting for you, Basil."

"I know. It's been tremendously unfair. And to go on like nothing has happened would just be an extension of the injustice."

Basil wasn't saying see you later—he was saying *goodbye.*

"I see," Ginger said. But she didn't see, not really. Basil had loved Ginger when Emelia was alive, but not now that she was dead?

No that couldn't be the case, Ginger thought. He must never have really loved her.

"Well, have a pleasant journey, Basil," she said,

proud to be in possession of the British stiff upper lip. "You'll understand if I don't see you to your motorcar."

"Ginger—"

Ginger held up a palm. "Please. Don't say anything more. Goodbye, Inspector." She left Basil standing on the front step and carried herself with dignity up the staircase until she reached her bedroom.

Boss had made his way upstairs at some point and watched her from his spot at the foot of her bed as she stood in the middle of the carpet, frozen in one place, staring out of the window, but not seeing.

It wasn't the image of Basil that flashed through her mind but Daniel, her dear lost husband. Oh, how she missed him!

She made quick strides to the bedside table and opened the drawer. Gingerly, she removed the black and white photo of Lieutenant Daniel Gold.

She stroked his image. "How can I blame Basil for being in love with his late wife when I'm still in love with you?"

Easing herself onto the edge of the bed, Ginger held the photo close to her heart. Despite her determination to stay emotionally strong, a tear rolled down her cheek. Sometimes it felt impossible to move on. Blast Daniel for dying, and blast Basil for leaving!

Boss traipsed over to her side, whined, and licked her face.

"Oh, Bossy. I can always count on you, can't I?"

The Boston terrier shook his stub of a tail in agreement. His big brown eyes stared up, full of unconditional love as if to say, "It's going to be okay."

Ginger scrubbed him behind the ears. "I know it is, Boss. I know."

Lizzie knocked on the door. "Telephone call for you, madam."

Ginger really didn't feel like taking a call. "Who is it?"

"Reverend Hill, madam." Lizzie's face flushed crimson. She'd carried a torch for the vicar as well and had suffered some embarrassment over it in the past.

Ginger put Boss down and propped the photograph of Daniel on her bedside table. She really ought to get a telephone put in the library so she wouldn't have to traipse all the way downstairs to her study whenever a call came in.

She paused to get her breath before saying hello.

Oliver's voice crossed the wires loudly. "Please forgive me for calling instead of coming to see you in person. My week is rather booked up but I have some news, and I wanted you to hear it from me."

Somehow Ginger knew what he was about to say. Why else would Oliver sound so cheery, even more so than usual? Oh, mercy. Was this why Louisa was being so cheeky?

"What is it, Oliver?"

"I'm getting married!"

Ginger gulped. "To *whom*?"

IF YOU ENJOYED READING *Murder at Kensington Gardens* please help others enjoy it too.

- **Recommend it:** Help others find the book by recommending it to friends, readers' groups, discussion boards and by suggesting it to your local library.
- **Review it:** Please tell other readers why you liked this book by reviewing at your point of purchase or on Goodreads. If you do write a review, let me know at **leestraussbooks@gmail.com** so I can thank you.
- **Suggest it** to your local librarian.

THIS BOOK HAS BEEN EDITED and proofed, but typos are like little gremlins that like to sneak in when we're not looking. If you spot a typo, please report it to: **admin@leestraussbooks.com**

SIGN UP for Lee's readers list (see website) and gain access to Ginger Gold's private Journal. Find out about Ginger's Life before the SS Rosa and how she became the woman she has. This is a fluid document that will cover her romance with her late husband Daniel, her time serving in the British secret service during World War One, and beyond. Includes a recipe for Dark Dutch Chocolate Cake!

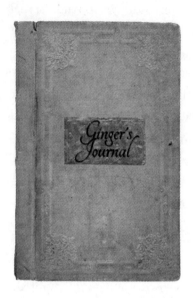

It begins: **July 31, 1912**

How fabulous that I found this Journal today, hidden in the bottom of my wardrobe. Good old Pippins, our English butler in London, gave it to me as a parting gift when Father whisked me away on our American adventure so he could marry Sally. Pips said it was for me to record my new adventures. I'm ashamed I never even penned one word before today. I think I was just too sad.

This old leather-bound journal takes me back to

that emotional time. I had shed enough tears to fill the ocean and I remember telling Father dramatically that I was certain to cause flooding to match God's. At eight years old I was well-trained in my biblical studies, though, in retro-spect, I would say that I had probably bordered on heresy with my little tantrum.

The first week of my "adventure" was spent with a tummy ache and a number of embarrassing sessions that involved a bucket and Father holding back my long hair so I wouldn't soil it with vomit.

I certainly felt that I was being punished for some reason. Hartigan House—though large and sometimes lonely—was my home and Pips was my good friend. He often helped me to pass the time with games of I Spy and Xs and Os.

"Very good, Little Miss," he'd say with a twinkle in his blue eyes when I won, which I did often. I suspect now that our good butler wasn't beyond letting me win even when unmerited.

Father had got it into his silly head that I needed a mother, but I think the truth was he wanted a wife. Sally, a woman half my father's age, turned out to be a sufficient wife in the end, but I could never claim her as a mother.

Well, Pips, I'm sure you'd be happy to know that things turned out all right here in America.

DON'T miss *Murder at St. George's Church!*

Book 7 in A Ginger Gold Mystery Series

Weddings can be murder ...

ROMANCE IS in the air for the delightful Reverend Oliver Hill. Unfortunately, the wedding rehearsal ends abruptly with the sudden and disturbing appearance of a body.

War widow fashionista Ginger Gold is determined to find the killer even if it means working with the dashing, yet exasperating Chief Inspector Basil Reed, but only in her professional capacity as a private investigator. Like they say: once burnt, twice shy.

Basil has his work cut out for him if he wants to solve this case *and* win back Ginger's heart.

He's up for the challenge.

www.leestraussbooks.com

LOVE the fashions of the 1920s? Check out Ginger Gold's Pinterest Board!

Join my Facebook readers group for fun discussions and first-to-know exclusives!

DID you know you can follow your favorite authors on Bookbub? If you subscribe to Bookbub.com — (and if you don't, why don't you? - They'll send you daily emails alerting you to sales and new releases on just the kind of books you like to read!) — follow me to make sure you don't miss the next Ginger Gold Mystery!

BB Follow on BookBub

ABOUT THE AUTHOR

Lee Strauss is the bestselling author of The Ginger Gold Mysteries series (cozy historical mystery), A Nursery Rhyme Suspense series (Mystery Sci-fi Romantic Suspense), The Perception series (young adult dystopian), and young adult historical fiction. When she's not writing or reading she likes to cycle, hike and kayak. She loves to drink caffè lattes and red wines in exotic places, and eat dark chocolate anywhere.

She also writes younger YA fantasy as Elle Strauss and sweet inspirational romance as Hope Strauss.

For more info on books by Lee Strauss and her social media links visit leestraussbooks.com. To make sure you don't miss the next new release, be sure to sign up for her readers list!

www.leestraussbooks.com
leestraussbooks@gmail.com

BOOKS BY LEE STRAUSS

On AMAZON

The Perception Series (YA dystopian/sci-fi/romance)

Playing with Matches (WW2 history/romance)

A Nursery Rhyme Suspense (Mystery Thriller)

Gingerbread Man

Life is but a Dream

Hickory Dickory Dock

Twinkle Little Star

Ginger Gold Mysteries (Cozy Historical)

Murder on the SS Rosa

Murder at Hartigan House

Murder at Bray Manor

Murder at Feathers & Flair

Murder at the Mortuary

Murder at Kensington Gardens

Murder at St. George's Church

ACKNOWLEDGMENTS

It takes a village to raise a child and a literary village to birth a book. Many thanks to my "villagers," Angelika Offenwanger, Heather Belleguelle, Connie Leap, Norm Strauss, Shadi Bleiken, Tom Reale and the folks at Brown Book publishing, and most recently, Molly C. Quinn of *Castle* fame!

My IRL (in real life) villagers, my parents Gene and Lucille Franke; husband Norm Strauss; kids Joel & Shadi, Levi, Jordan and Tasia; and my close friends, Donna, Shawn, Norine, Lori, and Marie - thanks for keeping me sane and grounded.

To YOU, dear reader for even reading these acknowledgments. Without you, I wouldn't be writing a page like this. Thank you for loving Ginger Gold and for joining along for the ride!

And as always I'm thankful to God for his mercies that are new every morning.